Milo's Wolves

In memory of
Francis, my father
and for David,
the father of my children
with love

CONTENTS

CONTENTS

PART ONE

The unknown brother

1

The unknown brother

I wouldn't like you to get the wrong idea. Milo's wolves don't have tails and fangs, and they don't go in for moonlight howling. Milo's wolves are more like the nine lives a cat's supposed to have (though ours only had one).

Milo McCool is my father, and Mary is my mother. It was Mary who told us about the wolves. Apparently, there was this very famous athlete in Ancient Greece called Milo. When he was getting on a bit he tried to tear an oak tree apart and got his hand stuck in it. The wolves ate him up before he could free himself. (What I'd like to know is, where were all his friends when he needed them?)

Our Milo isn't an athlete, but in his head he is. Our Milo is an actor who doesn't work very often. He used to be in a television series about undercover cops – *The Dark Knights* – and he did most of his own stunts. They were quite dangerous and Milo broke just about every bone in his body. Plus he burnt his hair (which is still very abundant, I'm glad to say), dislocated his shoulder, broke two teeth and smashed his knee. I don't know how many wolves it took to polish off ancient Milo, but Dad's certainly broken the cat's record.

Mum says that every injury was like one of those

wolves biting into Milo's flesh. Until, just before the last bite, *The Dark Knights* ended, and Milo was left all chewed up and with nowhere to go, but at least not dead. Nobody wanted an ex-Dark Knight with broken teeth and a bit of a limp. The world of entertainment turned its back. So Milo stayed at home and looked after us: Andy who's twelve, me, Laura, I'm eleven, and Polly who's seven. Mary went back to work with a tour operator, arranging wonderful trips for other people. And the wolves stayed away.

Milo was the best kind of house-father. He rarely bothered us with stuff like tidying rooms or wearing the right clothes. Shopping was an adventure because he always lost the grocery list, and cooking was a game because he hated sticking to recipes. He didn't always remember to change the bed-linen and the ironing was a bit hit and miss (like burnt sleeves and creases in the wrong places) but he would read stories far into the night, until we all fell asleep in a heap. My favourite was *The Little Prince*. I always thought the author was a saint. Dad patiently explained that it was just his name, Antoine de Saint-Exupéry, but he was still a saint to me, and whenever I was troubled I would talk to him, just as if he were standing quietly beside me. I still do.

The neighbours called our garden an eyesore, but we loved it. It was quite wild and the only tree, a huge sycamore, was hung with wind-chimes and tyres and swinging ladders. The games Milo invented were legendary. We spent a great deal of time in the garden, playing with cats and rabbits and a stray dog or two. Once, we found someone's cobra, dozing in the sun, and once a monkey. But we never saw a wolf. And then Gwendal arrived, trailing a whole pack of them, and our lives changed forever.

It was Saturday morning so we were all at home. Mum called us into the kitchen and I noticed her voice had a nervous edge to it, as though she were a little afraid. I was there first because her tone intrigued me, Polly came in from the garden and then Andy walked through the door, backwards, with a rat on each foot. He called his rats Snow and Flake; they were white, as you might have guessed, and both male, so Andy said. He was wrong. When he bought them Mum had made a condition: same sex, no offspring. Who could blame Andy for a little white lie? He loved those rats.

Mum was sitting at the end of the table, and Dad stood behind her with his hand on her shoulder. They looked as though they had been posed by a Victorian photographer.

'Sit down,' Mum said.

We sat in our usual places round the table, and then Mum plunged straight in. No hints, clues, gentle pre-ambles. No shock-absorbers. Just, 'Your brother's coming home today. We thought we ought to prepare you.'

That was preparation? We were stunned. Milo smiled encouragingly, but we weren't encouraged.

Milo said, 'We thought we should tell you before he arrived. So you could get used to the idea.'

'We haven't got long,' I remarked. My own voice sounded distant, as though my ears were blocked.

Andy had always wanted a brother, but he didn't look as if he wanted this one. His eyebrows had crashed together in a heavy black line above his nose.

Polly asked a sensible question. 'Where's he been?'

'Been?' said Mum.

'Until now,' I clarified.

'Oh! Oh, away.'

'We gathered that.' I pulled together all the jangly threads of questions that had been whizzing round my brain. 'But why's he been away? Why didn't we know about him? Where's the evidence of his existence in this family? How old is he? What's his name? What . . .'

'Wait, Laura!' Dad came to Mum's rescue. 'I'll tell you everything.'

Why did I feel that Dad wouldn't tell us the most important, the most shocking thing of all? I always knew when Dad wasn't telling the truth. I'm afraid this happened rather often. I wouldn't say he told lies deliberately. It was just that, from time to time, Milo had found it necessary to tell stories. Like the time Alfie, the cat, had been run over and Milo said a nice woman had taken him to live with her. Like the time Mum crashed the car and he said she'd gone to see a friend and swapped cars. Worst of all when Gran died, Milo said she'd gone to America. He came clean eventually, because we had to go to the funeral, and it would have been embarrassing if we hadn't known who we were burying.

Dad's eyes are a greeny-grey, like seawater, but when he's telling stories i.e. lies, they turn a bright mossy green. We watched him carefully, waiting for the sea change.

'He's nine,' Milo began, 'so he comes between Laura and Polly.' I'd always wondered why there were four years between me and Polly, while Andy and I had been squeezed together. 'His name is Gwendal.'

'What kind of a name is that?' Andy muttered.

'The hero in a book I was reading when he was born,' Mum said. 'I can't remember the title.'

Now the storytelling gleam came into Dad's eyes. 'When Gwendal was six months old, he was very, very ill. So ill we thought he'd die.'

'What was it called? His illness?' I asked.

'Ah . . . a bone ailment,' Dad searched for a name. 'Osteo . . . osteo . . .' Mum couldn't help him. 'I can't pronounce it,' he smiled.

I couldn't bring myself to ask how this disease might be spelled. I knew it didn't exist because Milo's eyes were now positively emerald.

'He had to go to hospital,' Dad went on, 'and that's where he's been ever since. We never mentioned it because we thought he'd never come . . . that he'd never recover.'

'To spare you the disappointment,' Mum said.

'But now he's been given the all clear,' Dad said, 'and he's coming home today.'

'So where's he going to sleep?' asked Polly.

'We were coming to that. I'll show you.'

We followed Dad upstairs and stopped behind him outside the door to the spare room. 'Ta-da!' He flung the door open.

We gazed into a room that was quite unrecognizable. White machinery gleamed on metal shelves: a computer, a printer, tape deck and copier. Silver-shaded lamps leaned obligingly over the bed and a chrome-covered desktop, and a pale thick-piled rug stretched from door to window.

'Not very practical for a boy,' Polly remarked, staring at the rug.

'You did all this while we were at school,' Andy accused Milo. 'And we never noticed. We weren't even curious.'

I made a mental note to be more curious in future. 'All that stuff,' I said. 'Why him?'

'He won't be going to school for a while,' Dad explained, a little guiltily, 'He's rather clever.'

'How come?' Andy's brows re-knitted themselves. 'We're not clever, none of us.'

'I wouldn't go that far,' Dad protested. 'You haven't really tried, Andy. And Polly might be one day. Laura has great imagination.'

Milo's gene, I thought.

'And you're all very healthy,' Dad declared. 'Rudely so, if I may say.'

'That's not the same at all,' I pointed out. 'Genius isn't in the same category as health.'

For some reason Dad didn't argue with that. So Gwendal was a genius, was he? It was suddenly all too awesome to contemplate. A brother: someone who'd never existed, plummeting into the heart of our family without any warning. Like magic. We gazed in silence at the bright, impersonal room, all our arguments knocked out of us.

Andy said, 'I still don't understand.' He ran downstairs, and we heard him pull his bike out of the porch. The gate crashed behind him.

Dad raised his eyebrows. 'I didn't a manage that very well,' he murmured.

Polly shook her head. 'It's all too much. How can we get used to it in just one day? You should have told us earlier.' She went into her room and closed the door.

Glancing at my father's troubled face, I said, 'You did your best.'

'Thanks, Lo!' (Lo was his name for me, sometimes.) He gave me a grateful smile. We were very close, Dad and me.

Mum hadn't moved from the kitchen. Even her expression hadn't changed. 'If only . . . if only they'd let us know six months ago,' she said.

'The hospital?' I asked. 'Maybe they didn't know that Gwendal would get better so suddenly.'

'No . . .' I thought she was going to tell me something, but she changed her mind and said, 'He'll fit in, Laura, I promise you. He's gentle and good-natured. In a few weeks you'll feel you've always known him. He's that sort of boy.'

She knew very well what sort of boy he was, but she wasn't ready to let me into their secret. Not for the first time, I wondered where the real Mary was hiding. She had to be this incredibly organized and beautiful person, and we loved her for it, but I knew that deep inside her there was someone she had never allowed us to see.

He arrived later that afternoon. Mum had begged us all to stay and welcome him, but Andy said he had a football match that he wouldn't miss for anyone, even a long-lost brother. It was up to Polly and me.

How do you wait for someone you've never known? Someone who's about to change the shape of your family? It was such an entirely new experience. Not the same as waiting for Gran or an auntie to arrive. Not at all the same as waiting for a friend.

Polly took Lancelot, the rabbit, into her room for some quality time. I just pottered, and then almost forgot Gwendal. It was only by chance that I was sitting by my bedroom window when the car drove up. It was a sleek, black, executive-style vehicle, and it purred beside the kerb while the door of the passenger seat opened. A boy got out, and then a woman in a plain blue suit. She didn't take the boy's hand, she just tapped him on the shoulder and led him through our gate. As I watched him walk up the path, I had the impression that an area of emptiness surrounded him. I can't explain it any better.

He was in no way remarkable. His hair was sparrow-brown, his face pale, but not unnaturally so. Seen from above his features looked small and pinched. He wore white jeans and a black anorak, and he carried a small case. Not a bag. This, I suppose, was a little unusual.

When I went downstairs, Mum had just opened the door and was talking to the woman in the blue suit. So I was there to welcome Gwendal as he took his first step into our home. His home.

'Hullo!' I put on the smile I'd been told was warm and friendly.

Gwendal didn't respond. Perhaps he didn't know how to. I wondered if he'd lived abroad, and if I should try French or German. '*Bonjour*,' I said.

Gwendal frowned.

'This is Laura,' Mum bent to kiss his cheek. Still he said nothing.

Dad came into the hall and gave Gwendal a hug. 'Welcome, Gwendal. Let me take your case.'

Gwendal gazed at Milo as if he were a kind of god, but

he clung to the handle of the case, and now I noticed the gleaming clasps and shiny black fittings, the flawless silver-ribbed sides and the slim coded lock. It looked like a case made for a weapon, not a boy's possessions. And as Milo drew Gwendal into the kitchen I saw how well-pressed he was, with his spotless jeans and a glint of silver in his silky black anorak.

He sat at the kitchen table, still hugging his case, and Mum said, 'You like coke, don't you? Better than tea and coffee.'

Gwendal nodded slowly. And Polly came in with Lancelot in her arms.

'A rabbit,' breathed Gwendal.

'Hullo, I'm Polly,' said Polly. 'And this is Lancelot. I think he needs a pee but you can come out and see him when you've had your tea.' She whisked Lancelot away, saying, 'He's not just mine, he's a family rabbit, so he's yours too.'

As I pulled out a chair beside Gwendal, he turned such a grim face to me that I almost stopped. And then I realized that the fierce glitters in his eyes were tears, and that he was trying hard to keep them from spilling over.

'Have you ever had a rabbit?' I asked, hoping that the tears would somehow tip back behind Gwendal's large blue eyes.

He shook his head and I thought, perhaps he's never had anything. Nothing with fur or teeth and claws. Perhaps he's only had hard, shiny unconscious things, such as the object that might be hidden in that sinister-looking case. I said, 'When Andy comes back, he'll show you his rats. They live in his room. He's crazy about them.'

'Thank you,' Gwendal said, blinking furiously. He stood the case beside his chair, the handle still within reach.

'Here,' Dad put a plate in front of him. There were two pieces of cake on it: chocolate and carrot. 'How about you, Laura?'

I heard the question, but I was thinking too hard about something else to reply.

'What's the matter?' Dad said. 'Have I grown horns or something?'

I found I was staring at Dad. There was no resemblance between Gwendal and my father. Nothing. Not a hint. Dad has wild hair like a brush. His face is broad with high cheek-bones and a wide, sensual mouth (so I've been told). He also has the aforementioned green eyes. I myself am the spitting image of Milo, except for the most important ingredient, the green eyes. Polly has those. 'Just carrot cake for me,' I said, and turned my attention to my mother.

Mary's red hair is smooth and shiny, like Andy's. They both have freckles, and so does Polly. In Polly's case the red is a bit watered down, more amber. I've always taken an interest in these things. It ruined my friendship with Sarah Drinkwater. When I mentioned the features she shared with Mr Connolly, the Art teacher, Mrs Drinkwater ejected me from their house rather brusquely. Milo said, 'No smoke without fire,' when I told him about it.

I looked at Gwendal. He didn't share one single feature with either of my parents. I think he found my gaze a bit disconcerting. He swallowed his coke rather fast, touched each piece of cake and then let his hand fall into his lap.

'If you're not hungry yet, Gwendal, don't worry.' Mum put an arm round his shoulders. 'Do you want to see your room?'

Gwendal nodded vigorously, picked up his case and followed Mum out of the kitchen.

'He's not our brother,' I stated, as soon as they were gone.

Caught off guard Dad cleared his throat and said, 'Well . . .'

'Don't, Dad.' I spoke before the lights in Milo's eyes went green. 'I know he's not. He's not one tiny bit like any of us. If you wanted to foster someone why didn't you say? We wouldn't have minded. I think it's a great idea.'

'It's not like that, Laura. He is your brother.'

'You mean you adopted him?'

'No. I mean that if Gwendal belongs anywhere, it's here.'

This was too much of a mystery, and it made me feel afraid for Gwendal. 'It doesn't make sense. What do you mean "if he belongs anywhere"? It sounds like he's an alien.'

For a fraction of a second I had the uncanny feeling that I'd almost hit upon the truth. It hardly diminished when Dad said, 'You'll be telling me next that he came from planet B-612.' (The little prince's planet).

Mum came back looking relieved. 'He likes it,' she said. 'Loves it, in fact. Thank goodness we got it right.' She sank into the chair beside Dad, who gave her shoulder an affectionate squeeze.

'How did you pay for all that stuff?' I asked. 'I mean we're not exactly rich.'

'Gwendal's funded,' Dad said quickly. 'An allowance.' His eyes glinted green as rain-washed grass. 'He has a sponsor.'

'Because he's clever?' I said suspiciously.

'You could say that,' Dad affirmed.

'He's not our brother, is he, Mum?' I said.

Mum looked at Dad. He raised his eyebrows, giving nothing away.

'Of course he is,' she said.

That made me angry. 'You'll never make me believe it,' I told them. I felt offended that they should try and trick us like that. I left them and went into the garden just in time to help Polly catch Lancelot before he squeezed under the fence.

'He doesn't seem like a brother, does he?' said Polly, bundling Lancelot into his run.

'Not in the least,' I agreed. 'But they say he is. So we'd better believe it for now. He's left all his cake, if you're hungry,' I added.

She skipped indoors to polish off Gwendal's portion of cake, and I thought, everything will be divided into four now. And I couldn't help feeling that it was unfair. Why should we have our portions decreased because of some-one who wasn't . . . who couldn't belong to us. Someone whom our parents had seen fit to lie about. For the first time in my life I found myself mistrusting Milo and Mary. It was horrible and I didn't know how to deal with it. Who was Gwendal? And why were Mum and Dad lying about him?

I'll ask him, I thought. But perhaps Gwendal didn't know who he was. Perhaps he was as much in the dark as I was. In times of stress I always went to the swing. And I sat there, swaying under the sycamore until I felt ready for the next step. I began to talk to Saint-Exupéry, and then of course, the little prince came into my mind, the boy who fell to earth from planet B-612.

When I went in, Polly's friend Zoe had arrived with hand-me-downs. Zoe was a good four inches taller than Polly, and rich. We were poor. Girly chatter resounded from the living-room as I scuttled past.

'Laura, come and see!' called Polly.

'Not now.' I hurried up the stairs.

Someone had hung a big silver G on Gwendal's door. Mum, as it turned out. I could hear Gwendal talking, his voice very low and urgent. So who was in there with him?

Without knocking I opened the door. Taken by surprise, Gwendal turned to me, his eyes wide and fearful. There were several strange-looking objects on the bed beside him: strips of metal, tiny screws, batteries, chips, and a thing like a mobile phone, with four ball-bearings at one end.

'Oh,' I said. 'Were you talking to yourself?'

'Not exactly,' he mumbled.

I saw the head. It sat in his cupped hands, a roundish thing, like a satsuma cut in half, only black. There were two hollow sockets where, perhaps, eyes should be, and in the centre of the 'face' a triangular chip like a nose. Set beneath this was a long squashed oval filled with dark glittering material.

'What on . . . what is it?' I asked. I had the oddest sensation that the eyeless head was watching me.

'He's Isidore. I haven't fixed him yet,' Gwendal said sharply.

'I'm sorry. Shall I go?' I felt as though I'd intruded on some very private ritual.

'No, it's all right,' he said. 'You can help me, if you like.'

I sat beside Gwendal and took a closer look at the head. Gwendal glanced at me, and said, 'He can see you, even though we haven't put his eyes in yet. And when I've fixed his body, he can record your voice, and film you!'

'Oh!' I looked bravely into the hollows of Isidore's face.

'This is my sister,' Gwendal told the head.

I was about to deny this, but in Gwendal's presence I couldn't. So I said, 'He has another sister, Polly, and a brother called Andy.'

'The head made a grating noise and I jumped.

'Message received,' Gwendal smiled. 'But not recorded, yet.'

Seeing that we were getting on so well, me and Isidore, Gwendal put the head into my hands and stood up. 'He'll look better with his eyes in,' he said. 'You can choose the colour. Blue, violet, yellow, amber, green or red?'

I almost said that the choice sounded like a set of traffic lights, but I managed to stop myself. I turned the head this way and that. It was very light.

'Well?' said Gwendal.

I remembered I'd been asked to make a choice. But eyes? Such a personal feature needed careful consideration. 'Green,' I said at last.

'Green?' Gwendal sounded doubtful. 'He's never worn green before.'

'Our father's eyes are green,' I said indignantly. 'I wouldn't propose just anyone could have green eyes.'

'Mmmm!' went Isidore. It was a hollow, almost human, sound.

'He feels favoured,' Gwendal said in a polite voice.

'Mmmm! Aaaah!' Isidore had a vocabulary.

'Let's put the eyes in,' I said. 'He looks a bit scary with those holes in his head.'

Gwendal took a small tin out of his silver case. The lid was marked 'Lenses'. He sat on the bed, opened the tin and poured its contents on to the duvet. An array of jewel-like marbles winked up at me, their shiny surfaces reflecting each other's brilliance.

'Aren't they pretty!' I exclaimed, before I had time to think of something more appropriate.

'I've got lenses, too. Contact lenses. But mine are transparent, not pretty. I'm myopic, you know. Short-sighted.' He solemnly removed two green marbles from the pile and placed them, one by one, into the sockets in Isidore's face. There was a small click as each one slid home.

'There!' said Gwendal. 'They're camera lenses really,' the eyes lit up, 'and they shine at night.'

Isidore looked exotic now, and rather inquisitive.

I said, 'Can I talk to you alone, Gwendal? I mean, can you turn Isidore off?'

I know it wasn't my imagination when the green marbles gave me a sparky sort of glare.

'It would be easier to turn myself off,' Gwendal said.

'Isidore is permanently on alert. The batteries in his head have renewable energy. He's indestructible. Immortal. He doesn't sleep. Anyway I wouldn't want him turned off. He's my guardian, my friend.'

'I see.' I glanced at the head. 'Who made him?'

'I did.'

'You?'

'Well, he was my idea, but I had advice from my sponsor,' Gwendal admitted.

'Who?'

'My sponsor. The person who supports me financially.' Gwendal began to gather the rest of Isidore into his lap: the coils and chips and the mobile phone body. 'Isidore won't interfere if you want to talk to me.'

His voice sounded just like any other nine year old boy's, but beneath the surface there seemed to be another voice, very wise and almost old.

'I'd like to know where you've been and what you've been doing all your life, up until now,' I said. 'And I'd like to know why you appeared in our house so suddenly.'

Gwendal pushed the robot-mobile's head into its body, and sighed. 'I had a crisis. *They* called it a crisis. I didn't want to be where I was any more. I didn't want to be anywhere.'

'You were very ill, weren't you?'

'Not ill. Not really ill. Just at risk.'

'What from?'

'I don't know. It's just what they told me.'

'Who's they?' I couldn't help pushing. It's just my nature. I've always wanted to know too much.

18

'The people where I was,' said Gwendal. 'Didn't your . . . didn't our parents tell you?'

'I'm afraid Dad enjoys telling lies,' I said. 'Stories,' I amended. 'A green light comes into his eyes and we know he's enjoying himself. The light came on when he told us about you.'

Gwendal considered this and then he smiled. 'I have a lot of data on Milo,' he said.

What an unusual word for a son to use of his father. But then there was nothing usual about the situation.

'So are *you* going to tell me the truth?' I asked.

Before he could reply a distant shriek caused him to start. 'Who's that?'

'Polly.' I went to open the door. 'It's probably nothing. She's very emotional.'

'My jacket,' came the outraged cry. 'I hate those rats. I hate them.'

'Sorry, Polly.' Andy had evidently come home. I could hear him pounding up the stairs. 'But don't blame Flake. It's . . .'

'Andy's rats have eaten Polly's clothes again,' I told Gwendal. 'But she will leave them on the floor.' I stepped on to the landing just in time to see Flake crawl over the lip of the staircase. I ran towards him, ready to pounce.

'Catch him, Laura!' yelled Andy. 'Or mum'll kill him.'

My hand swept down. Too late. Flake swerved past me and ran on. I turned to see the white rat hesitate. Gwendal had followed me on to the landing and now stood very still, looking down at Flake. The rat made a very imaginative decision. He ran straight at Gwendal, up his leg, over his sweater, up and up until he reached

Gwendal's neck. Once there, he closed his eyes and clung. If he could have spoken I'm sure he'd have said, 'Home. Can't catch me now.' Gwendal seemed to have been turned to stone.

'Well done,' said Andy. He approached Gwendal and put out his hand. 'Hi! I'm Andy. You're Gwendal, aren't you?'

Gwendal said nothing. His eyes were like saucers.

'Don't be scared. He won't hurt you,' Andy said gently. He carefully removed Flake from Gwendal's neck.

'You won't hurt him will you?' Gwendal's voice shook.

' 'Course not,' said Andy. 'It wasn't his fault. I'm supposed to put them in a cage when I go out, but I forgot. It's his nature to chew things.'

It was an unusual way for a boy to meet his long-lost brother, but the odd situation seemed to settle round them quite comfortably.

'Look!' Polly appeared, holding up a bright blue jacket. 'Look at it!' She said this with a sob, which wasn't surprising because little nibbled inroads had been made all round the cuffs of each sleeve.

'It's a nice jacket,' Gwendal said.

'*Was* nice,' said Polly with feeling. 'Now it's ruined.'

'No,' said Gwendal. 'It could still look very good. If you slashed the rest of the cuffs with scissors, to make a sort of fringe, it would look really cool.'

Polly stared, first at Gwendal, then at the jacket. 'You're right. Gwendal, you're a genius.' She ran down-stairs with a whoop.

Gwendal gave a strangely practised smile and went back to his room.

'So that's our brother,' Andy said quietly.

'If you can believe it,' I murmured.

'I can't. He's just not a McCool, is he?'

'And it's got nothing to do with him being away for the whole of his life until now, has it?'

Andy murmured, 'He seems alien. But somehow OK!'

'Why did they lie to us?' I knew Andy couldn't answer that.

'Perhaps the truth is too complicated,' he suggested.

'Or someone has sworn them to secrecy.' How could I have guessed that I had hit upon the truth?

2

The first wolf

When the first wolf appeared, Polly was alone with Gwendal. She told me what happened later. Much later.

She'd had a row with her best friend Jessica Tilly, and she was crying when Milo arrived to collect her from school, so he made her tell him all about it.

Jessica's father had recently taken to wearing a patch over one eye, and Polly had suggested he looked like a pirate. Unfortunately the eye operation Mr Tilly had undergone had been rather harrowing for his family, so I wasn't surprised to hear that Jessica couldn't see the funny side of it.

Milo could, of course, having spent a great deal of his time in bandages. He began to laugh. 'Shall I ring Mrs Tilly and make an excuse for you?' he wanted to know.

Polly had made him promise not to make things worse. 'No,' she said. 'No lies. They don't work.'

Milo saw Polly into the house, made her a marmalade sandwich and then ran out for an evening paper.

Polly couldn't eat. The Jessica problem weighed heavily. How could she go to school tomorrow? How could she face angry, tearful Jessica? Everyone else was on Jessica's side. It wasn't fair. Polly hadn't meant to be unkind. She began to cry again.

'What's the matter?' Gwendal was staring at her from the doorway.

Polly was rather taken aback. She hadn't heard the approaching footsteps. She told Gwendal she'd had a row with her best friend. 'She'll never be my friend again,' she said.

Gwendal took a chair beside her and bit into the marmalade sandwich, while Polly explained what had happened.

'That's a funny way to lose a friend,' he remarked.

Polly said, 'It's not funny. Not a bit.'

Gwendal changed the subject. He asked Polly if she wanted the rest of the sandwich.

Polly said no. 'What shall I do about Jessica?' she asked.

'I've never had a row,' Gwendal said, 'so I wouldn't know.'

Polly was astonished. How could anyone possibly live for nine years without having a row?

'I've had arguments,' he amended, 'disagreements. But not a row.'

Polly stared at Gwendal. She began to realize that he didn't fit. His neat head, his cool blue eyes and his careful hands – they were not at home in our cluttered, scruffy kitchen. It was almost as if Gwendal were not really there. It gave Polly the creeps.

'In that place . . .' she began, 'in that hospital where you were. Weren't there any children?'

'It was a clinic,' he told her. 'Sometimes there were

children, but not for long. There were always animals.'

'Animals? Why?' she asked.

'Experiments,' he said. He went to the sink, rinsed his hands under the tap and walked out of the room.

He had been no help whatsoever. Polly felt let down. More than that, she felt uneasy. It dawned on her that she was alone in the house with Gwendal and she didn't like it. The garden seemed a safer place. She ran out and seized Lancelot from his run. He lay in her arms, his eyes closed while she gently stroked his nose. A lone seagull called above her, and she noticed how grey and grumpy the sky looked.

The wind was shaking autumn leaves off all the trees, and the wind-chimes on the sycamore began to peal. Polly let her gaze follow the line of the big tree, up and up until there, between two boughs she saw a lighted window. And in the window the dark figure of a boy. She couldn't see Gwendal's features but she knew that he was watching her.

Polly didn't hear the garden gate swing open, didn't hear the soft footfalls on the grass. She noticed that Gwendal's position had altered, and almost heard a sound come from him. Now he was struggling to open the window. Polly screwed up her eyes and strained to catch what he was saying. The window flew open and Gwendal pointed at something behind her. 'Polly!' he shouted.

Polly turned. Too late. A grey shape streaked past her. A long, misty-looking coat swept across the lawn, sending dead leaves whispering into the air.

Polly screamed and Lancelot leapt out of her arms.

I got home twenty minutes later than usual. I dumped

my bag in the hall and called up the stairs. 'Polly? Dad? Are you in?'

No response.

A door banged somewhere and a cold draught rushed into the hall. I walked through the sitting-room and found the french windows open.

'Polly?' I called.

Polly was not there. Nor, I noticed, was Lancelot. This was worrying. She wasn't in her room, or mine or Andy's. Neither were Andy's rats as far as I could see. This didn't seem important at the time. I was about to knock on Gwendal's door when Milo came in.

'Dad!' I ran downstairs.

'Anything the matter?' he asked, seeing my expression.

'Where is everyone? Polly's not here. Nor's . . .'

'Not here?' said Milo. 'Are you sure? I've only been gone . . .' He clutched his wind-tangled hair. 'Oh, my god. I suppose it's been half an hour or more, I got talking . . .'

'The back gate's open and Lancelot's disappeared,' I said.

'Then she's gone to find him.' Milo sounded more cheerful. 'I'll go and look for her.'

I wanted to go with him but he insisted I stay and wait for the others. 'Mum'll worry if no one's here,' he said.

'We could leave a note.'

'She'd worry even more.'

'There's Gwendal,' I said. 'He could explain.'

'Go and have a chat,' said Milo. 'I'll get the bike out.'

Dad's got an old and precious motorbike – a Norton – hidden in the garage. Mum's always afraid he'll take one of us to school on it, but he hasn't yet.

'How will you carry a rabbit on a motorbike?' I asked.

'Good point, Lo!' Dad left on foot.

I went up to Gwendal's room and found that the door was locked. 'Gwendal,' I called. 'Are you in there?'

The door was unlocked and swung back. Gwendal stared at me. He looked terrified. 'I'm sorry,' he said.

'Did you see what happened to Polly?'

He nodded miserably. 'It's my fault. The man . . . the grey man . . . he came for me. That's why I locked the door. I saw him coming. But Polly didn't.'

'The grey man?' I exclaimed. 'Has Polly been kidnapped?'

'No. She was just frightened. Lancelot ran away and she ran after him. The grey man left when I wouldn't talk to him. I said Milo would sort him out.'

It was just as I had thought, and yet I realized it was not merely a matter of Polly chasing a rabbit. A stranger was involved. Someone had invaded our home. 'Did you know this man?' I asked.

'Not exactly,' Gwendal hesitated, 'but I've seen him. He was often at the clinic. I saw him from the window, watching me. He never came in, though.'

'And you don't know who he is, or why he was watching you?'

Gwendal shook his head. 'I thought when I came here, he'd give up. But he must have traced me, somehow.'

I became aware that some frantic activity was taking place in Isidore.

'He gets so angry sometimes, he can't speak,' Gwendal explained. He suddenly thrust the little robot into my hands.

'Poor Isidore,' I found myself saying. 'It must hurt, all that noise inside your head.'

The robot's eyes rotated in a sort of blink. The clicking quietened and three words appeared on the tiny screen below his head. 'Report to sponsor.'

'He keeps saying that,' muttered Gwendal.

I said, 'Who is your sponsor?'

'The person who . . . well, my guardian, I don't know who he is, exactly. He wants me to talk to him.'

'So why don't you?'

'Why should I tell him everything? I'm free of him now. Free of everybody. They promised me. From now on it's just Milo, that's what they said. He's my father, he's all I need. I'm fed up with being watched.' He lay Isidore face down on the bed. 'Let's go.'

We left the room together and in the next few minutes the rest of our family began to arrive. Andy came first, but when I tried to tell him about Polly he seemed more concerned with his vanished rats.

I had more luck with Mum. 'Polly? Gone?' she cried. 'Where was your father? What was he thinking of?'

'It's all right, Mum. He's gone to find her. They'll be back soon.' I didn't mention the grey man. She had enough to contend with just then.

Gwendal paced nervously round the kitchen, until Mum grilled some pitta bread and made him sit down to eat it. His appetite had improved enormously since his first day at home. 'I've had a sandwich,' he told Mum. 'Polly's actually.'

'Never mind.' Mum's thoughts were obviously elsewhere.

'It's my fault,' Gwendal spoke decisively.

'Of course it's not,' she said.

He told her about the grey man.

'What on earth's going on?' Mum asked me.

'I don't know, Mum, but I'm sure things'll sort themselves out.' I wasn't sure, but I didn't know what else to say.

Outside the sky darkened. The sycamore thrashed against the fence in a sudden squall. The rush-hour traffic roared towards the motorway.

Mum and I kept busy in the kitchen. We decided that a crisp lasagne would be just the thing to greet two weary hunters.

'I've a good mind to cook a rabbit,' Mary muttered, 'just to serve Lancelot a lesson.'

That doesn't make sense, I thought. I gazed out at the glittery blur of headlights and shiny wet traffic, unable to draw the curtains against them, as if it might keep Polly and Milo from the safety of home.

'Where can they be?' Mary kept muttering. 'Why don't they just give up and come home? We can get another rabbit.'

At six o'clock the doorbell shrieked through the house. Mum tore to the front door and there was Polly, alone. Her face was blotchy with tears, her hands and clothes were covered in grime and her hair looked as though something were nesting in it.

'Polly!' Mum cried, pulling her into the hall with a hug.

'Where's Dad?' I said.

'And Lancelot,' added Andy.

Polly burst into tears.

'Didn't he find you? Where've you been?' Mum dragged Polly into the kitchen and sat her down with a drink. 'Are you hungry, darling? You must be.'

Polly shook her head, then nodded. She couldn't make up her mind what to say first. 'Lancelot went into the Underground,' she said at last.

'He caught a train, did he?' Andy's try for a smile didn't work.

'*In* the Underground, not *on* it!' Polly said fiercely.

'Which station?' Andy never gave up.

'I can't remember. No one could catch him. I asked them to help, but no one would, except a nice man who tripped on the up escalator and then fell down it.' She gulped and more tears spilled over her grimy cheeks.

'Never mind, darling,' Mum said.

'So where did Lancelot end up?' The question had to be asked, but Andy's tone didn't seem appropriate.

'He went onto the platform,' said Polly, 'and he jumped on to the track.' We all gasped. Andy opened his mouth, probably to say 'roasted rabbit', then thought better of it.

'I saw him,' Polly went on. 'Everybody saw him . . . they were pointing and looking and shouting . . . and somebody laughed.'

'How could they?' I muttered.

'And then he hopped into the tunnel,' said Polly.

'Oh, poor, poor Polly!' Mum rocked and smothered her with hugs.

'So Dad never found you,' I said.

'Oh, yes,' Polly's eyes began to swim again. 'We went into the Underground together.'

'So where is he now?' Mum asked.

'He went into the tunnel,' said Polly.

We stared at her, shocked and silent, and then Gwendal whispered, 'But . . . but couldn't he be electrocuted . . . or something?'

Mum groped for a chair and lowered herself into it. 'Are you sure?' she said faintly.

Polly nodded and nodded. In fact she couldn't seem to hold her head still at all.

'No!' groaned Mum. 'I don't believe it.' And then suddenly she changed her tune and angrily cried, 'How could he? How could he?'

How could he not, I thought? For weeks now I'd been aware of Milo's craving for dangerous activity. He'd been aching to jump off the bus before it stopped, longing to leap up six steps instead of one, yearning for a decent car-chase. But the role of responsible father had meant a lot to him. Now, at last, he could combine danger with responsibility.

Was it responsible to chase a rabbit into an Underground tunnel? There was bound to be at least one wolf down there.

3
The man in the grey fedora

Mum's natural good sense began to reassert itself. She too could be a person of action. 'The police,' she said. 'It's an offence to jump on the track, a criminal act. They'll know what's happened. I'll ring them.'

'Perhaps we should eat the lasagne,' Andy suggested. 'Or it'll burn,' he added lamely.

Mum went to phone the police while Andy dished out the lasagne. No one was hungry. Even Andy could only manage three mouthfuls when it came to it. He dropped his fork sighing, 'I've got indigestion now.'

We listened to Mum dialling. With every call her voice become more frantic. She rang London Under-ground, police enquiries, four different police stations, the RSPCA, the ambulance service and three hospitals. No one, it seemed, had any knowledge of a man and a rabbit in the Underground. In fact one rather unsym-pathetic police-man mentioned Alice in Wonderland.

'Someone must know!' Mum's desperate wail floated down the hall.

We stared at our plates of cooling lasagne, lost for

words. Gwendal began to look drained of life, as though every minute of Milo's absence made him less real himself.

At last Mum seemed to make contact with a voice that was more promising. 'You have!' Our spirits rose. 'His body?' We heard her say. 'Or himself. His body. I said his body!' she screeched. 'Oh, never mind.' She slammed down the receiver and came into the kitchen. 'There isn't a body!' she told us.

I found myself screaming.

'No! No, darling. It means Dad's alive,' Mum said. 'Somehow . . . somewhere. He was taken to the police station, but now he's out.'

'Aren't they going to bring him home?' asked Andy.

'I expect they're too busy,' Mum said absently.

'So we just have to wait,' I cried. 'He may be burnt, or cut, or . . . well, just injured.'

'Who knows?' Mum sighed and helped herself to lasagne.

'Leave some for Dad,' I said.

All at once the cold food seemed appealing, and we began to eat again. Though every mouthful dropped into my stomach like a bag of lead.

An hour passed and Mum's anger with Dad began to overwhelm her relief. He had no right, she kept repeating. How dare he? Who did he think he was? Superman?

'But Lancelot . . .' said Polly in Milo's defence, and Mum smiled helplessly.

I went to sit on the front step. A cold wind had whisked the rain away, but now a thin mist swathed the trees. The step was damp but I didn't care. I promised Mum I wouldn't move away from my post and she was too tired to argue.

I'd only been there a few minutes when Gwendal slipped out and sat beside me. 'I think he's safe,' he said.

I said, 'Yes,' to make myself feel better, as much as for Gwendal.

'I chose him,' he announced. It sounded as though it were a confession.

'I know,' I muttered. 'You said.' I kept my eyes on the road searching the darkness behind the mist. First one way, then the other.

'They came to see me,' he went on. 'Mum and Dad. Not often, not enough really. Then I saw the videos: *The Dark Knights*. And I knew that Milo could rescue anyone from anything.'

I suddenly thought of all the weekends, and the odd days, when Gran came to mind us, or Mum's cousin Dora. So that's where Milo and Mary had been; with their other child. It can't have been easy.

'How could you tell he wasn't just acting?' I asked. 'That he was really like that?'

'He was on a ladder, at the top and it fell, and he was under it.' Gwendal appeared to be describing a scene that he was actually watching, all over again. 'And there was a close-up and I knew he'd really fallen and was really hurt. And I thought, 'That's my father.''

But he's not your father, said a voice in my head. Yet I had no proof of this. Why did Gwendal need rescuing? And from what? At that moment a figure approached with a familiar swinging stride.

'Dad!' I yelled. I ran into the street with Gwendal close behind me.

Milo's eyes glittered in a face that was almost entirely black. His hair was a dark, oily tangle, his jacket was gone and his shirt more black than white.

'Careful,' he said as I flung my arms round him. He was carrying a large box which he handed to Gwendal. 'Lancelot,' he explained.

The others had heard me cry out and were already on the step when we lurched through the gate. There was such a clamour of amazed and delighted screams from our house that windows and doors banged open all down River street. A party or a murder, they must have wondered.

'You're still . . . you look like a coal-miner!' cried Mum, planting a sheaf of newspapers on the chair Milo was about to sit in. He sank on to the paper, still smiling, his teeth a startling white in his oily face.

I'd seldom seen my father look so happy. He couldn't hope to answer all our questions. How had he managed to avoid the lethal piece of track? How had he ducked beneath the speeding tons of metal? We would never really know if it was luck or judgement.

While we were still begging for answers, Gwendal opened the box and lifted Lancelot into his arms.

'Lancelot!' cried Polly. 'I love you.'

'Lethal rabbit,' Mary muttered.

Gwendal passed the rabbit to Polly and then, without a word, he went to the sink, filled a bowl with soapy water and brought it to Milo. 'For your hands,' he said.

That no one else had thought to do this caused a surprised silence.

'Thank you, Gwendal.' Milo gave Gwendal a very special smile, and Gwendal stared at Milo's face as though the smile were a lifeline.

'This family won't sleep tonight,' Mum warned. She still seemed torn between joy and fury. Her eyes were brimming when she pushed the cold lasagne in front of Milo.

'You didn't forget me,' Milo cried.

Mary smacked his oily shoulder.

I found myself yawning, and it started everyone off.

'Saturday tomorrow,' said Milo. 'We can sleep all day.'

'Oh, no you can't,' said Mary.

I could hardly keep my eyes open. I went to bed and fell asleep to the sound of Milo's bathroom singing. He was taking a mammoth bath, but I daresay he needed it. The water hurtled through the pipes behind my bed, on and on and on, along with the deep contented singing. It was as if an old and mischievous spirit had been reborn in Milo and he was celebrating its return.

I dreamed of a train, rushing out of the dark. As it sped past me I could see that my family was on board. They stared out at me, their faces bleached by the white strips of light. I could even see myself, holding tight to Gwendal. Where was he taking us? Where were they bound, he and Milo? And would they reach their destination before the wolves closed in?

It took a long time for Mum to forgive Milo. Next morning she banged round the house trying to avoid him. Andy did his fair share of banging too, in his desperate search for Flake. The house fairly shook with activity.

Eventually Andy had to abandon his quest in favour of football. Grabbing a Mars bar he was gone.

A few minutes later Polly found Flake. He (or rather she) had made a nest in one of Milo's slippers and produced seven babies.

'So now we've got nine rats,' said Polly happily.

'Nine!' Mum shrieked. 'I can't live with nine rats. Why couldn't Andy get a girlfriend or something. Why did it have to be rats?'

'Mum, he's only twelve,' said Polly.

'I had a girlfriend when I was twelve,' Milo murmured.

'You had one when you were four,' Mum rounded on Dad. 'You've always had one. Four at a time most probably.'

'I've loved you, and only you, from the moment I laid eyes on you,' Milo stated solemnly.

'Ah, but before that? And it was a long before,' Mum said with meaning. 'You were thirty-four when we married.'

It was a familiar story and one we loved: How mum and dad had met. He'd gone to a travel agency after one of his accidents. He was tired and in pain and needed a special sort of holiday. But the girl at the desk (Mary) had been so beautiful he kept going back for more and more brochures, until in the end he said, 'Really it's not just the holiday I need, it's you.' Mary, of course, knew very well who Milo was, and was already half in love.

So Polly and I knew scenes like these always ended happily. But Gwendal didn't. He watched the adults anxiously. The drama of Lancelot and the tunnel had rather eclipsed the excitement of his arrival. I suggested a walk. 'Gwendal hasn't got to know his way about yet,' I said.

'Where will you go?' Mum wanted to know.

I told her the park would be a good place to start. I promised to be no longer than an hour. Polly decided to join us, once she'd made Flake's maternity arrangements more comfortable.

It was a bleak, drizzly day. The trees in the park slipped through the mist, reaching for the sallow sky; slim unclimbable trees that spilled their tawny leaves in mysterious patterns on the path.

'We'll come to a lake soon,' Polly told Gwendal. She led him on to the grass where she kicked the leaves and threw them about like confetti. I felt a weight of responsibility I wasn't used to. Watching Gwendal I thought, he doesn't quite know how to play.

When we reached the lake we sat on a damp bench and watched the ducks for a while.

'They look happy, those ducks,' Gwendal remarked.

'They like wet weather,' said Polly. 'Do you like it, Gwendal? Where you've been, did you go out much?'

'No,' he said. 'I had PE sometimes, and a basketball with a net on the wall.'

'Who was your favourite person there?' Polly wanted to know everything.

Gwendal thought for a moment, and then he said, 'Dr Zeigler, but he wasn't there all the time. He was a consultant, I think. Sometimes, he took me to a different house, out in the country, and we'd have long talks, and walk about. Those were the best times. Sometimes, other children came to the clinic for treatment, but they always left. That's how we came up with Isidore, my sponsor and me. Isidore can't ever leave me.' Gwendal frowned up at the giant trees. 'After a while they stopped expecting me to die.'

'So why didn't you come home?' I asked.

'Because . . .' he took a breath. 'Because I don't exist.'

'Of course you exist.' I spoke rather harshly, shaken by the thought of sitting next to a ghost. 'Who said you didn't?'

Gwendal shook his head. 'I found out. I listened at doors. I don't exist on paper. I'm a secret.'

'Dad and Mum don't have secrets,' I protested, and then I realized that, of course, they did.

'They do,' said Polly.

I'd read that everyone in Britain has a number: every birth had to be registered, even babies who died; they all have an identity, an existence. I stared at Gwendal, wanting to reassure myself by touching him but not quite knowing how to. 'Of course you exist,' I repeated. 'And you're certainly not a secret now.'

'You're our brother,' Polly added.

'Yes,' Gwendal said gratefully.

We left the bench and walked on, round the lake and then on to another path. Here the trees grew so close to the verge that they made a dark, vaulted avenue, and again I thought of the tunnel that might have swallowed Milo.

The sun was making valiant efforts to break through the cloud, and now and again the mist would be lit by a hesitant gold sparkle. I couldn't be sure when I first became aware of the approaching figure. One moment the horizon was empty, and the next there he was: a shadowy form moving slowly towards us.

It was only a man in a grey hat, a fedora as it happened, but I found that I wanted to run from it. Gwendal had the same idea but as we both began to turn, Polly suddenly bounced forward, exclaiming, 'Look! Look, a pigeon. Poor thing, it can't fly!'

'Polly, come back,' I cried.

Why was the park so deserted suddenly? Where were the Saturday joggers, the dog-walkers, the duck-feeders? Where were the shoppers taking a short-cut into town? 'Polly!' I shrieked.

Polly was intent on rescue. She flew on, alighting like a bird herself, beside the injured pigeon. 'I think it's broken its wing,' she called. 'What shall I do?'

The dusky presence moved closer. It swelled, like a cloud, behind Polly on the ground, and Gwendal, clasping my arm, said, 'It's him. The grey man. Run, Laura. Please, run.'

'I can't leave Polly,' I said. 'You run.'

Gwendal seemed unable to move.

'Polly!' My voice came out like a screech. 'Run, quickly! It's him. The grey man.'

Polly got to her feet, the bird held between both hands. She looked behind her and leapt forward with a cry. But she couldn't get her balance, and with an awful howl, crashed on to the path again. The pigeon fluttered out of her hands and then lay still, its creamy feathers spread wide on the tarmac.

The stranger had reached Polly now. For a moment he

looked down at her and then, speaking in a quiet voice, he offered his hand. Polly took it and got up, rubbing her knees.

'We'll have to go back for her,' I told Gwendal.

'No,' he said.

'Gwendal, we have to.'

'No,' he muttered.

Polly pointed to the bird. The stranger stepped over to the awkward spray of feathers and picked it up. Polly smiled and began to lead the man towards us. We heard her say, 'This is my brother and sister.' She seemed quite happy in the man's company.

'Good morning!' The man lifted his hat as he approached.

Gwendal's fingers tightened on my arm. He moved so close to me I could feel the tremor that ran through his body. 'Don't,' he breathed. 'Don't!'

'Don't what?' I whispered. 'It'll be all right. We're in a public park. He can't do anything.'

The man's long face was creased and sallow; his hooded eyes were very small, but burned with such a brightness, they looked hardly human. Contact lenses, I thought, to comfort myself. No hair could be seen beneath the grey fedora, but there had been a glimpse of black when he briefly lifted it.

'Nathan Culfire,' said the man, extending his hand. His lips retained their meagre lines, and his smile betrayed no hint of teeth.

I found that I didn't want to give him my name, as though giving anything of myself away might weaken me somehow. But eventually I confessed that I was Laura. I wouldn't give him Gwendal's name, though. 'This is my brother,' I said.

Gwendal's grip threatened to bite through to my bone, when I added, 'I think you two already know each other.'

'Indeed!' Mr Culfire's second smile still showed no teeth. 'Though I haven't yet had the pleasure of a chat.'

'Well, thank you for helping Polly,' I said, trying to wrest my arm from Gwendal's frantic lock. 'We'd better get home now. We're late.'

'Can't you spare an old man a few minutes?' asked Mr Culfire, his eyes on Gwendal's face.

'I don't think so.' I tried to sound firm.

'Shame.' He retreated to a bench and sat down, stroking the pigeon's head. To my horror, Polly sat beside him.

'What will you do with the bird?' she asked.

'I'll take care of it.' Again the smile that was not a smile.

'Do you know how to mend wings?' Polly persisted. 'I mean are you an RSPCA person?'

'I'm not,' Mr Culfire confessed. 'As for wings . . . you could say I try to encourage them.'

'How?' asked Polly.

I found myself saying, 'What sort of wings can be encouraged?'

'Angels' wings,' said Mr Culfire.

All at once, Gwendal acquired a necessary ounce of courage. Stepping up to Mr Culfire, he said, 'You came into our house. I saw you. You trespassed.'

'An exaggeration, Gwendal,' Mr Culfire said sharply.

'The french windows were open. I merely came and called to you. But there was no answer.'

'No,' said Gwendal. 'Because I remember now, I've seen you before, haven't I? Outside the clinic. What do you want? Why don't you came right out and say it?'

'How does one tell a boy he's an angel?'

Gwendal stepped back as though from a blow, and then he began to run. I caught hold of Polly's hand and jerked her to her feet. 'We've got to stay with Gwendal,' I said.

'Boys aren't angels,' Polly commented as I dragged her away.

'I'll bring the bird,' Mr Culfire called, 'when it's recovered.'

'No,' I cried. 'Don't bother.' I made Polly run whether she wanted to or not.

'But . . . but . . .' Polly protested. 'I want . . .'

'Shut up!' I said.

To my relief Gwendal was waiting for us at the park gates. Without a backward glance, I said, 'Come on,' and we leapt into the safety of a busy street.

As soon as our house came into view, I left the others and ran the rest of the way down River Street.

'You look spooked,' said Andy when I burst into the kitchen. One of the rats, presumably Snow, was perched on his shoulder.

'Where's Dad?' I gasped for air. 'Something happened in the park.'

'What happened?' Milo backed out of the larder.

Polly and Gwendal had appeared and it was Polly who told Milo about Mr Culfire and the bird.

Milo seemed more amused than concerned, until I said, 'It was the man who was here before, the grey man.'

Dad's smile slipped for a moment, and when it returned it still held a trace of anxiety. 'There are some funny people about,' he said. 'I don't like you talking to them, you know that, Polly.'

'But the bird,' argued Polly. 'I had to.'

'You shouldn't have,' Gwendal said quietly. 'He's dangerous.'

'D'you think you should tell the police?' I asked Dad.

Milo lost his smile again. 'No,' he said uncertainly.

It began to dawn on me that there were secrets about Gwendal's life that had to remain hidden even from the police.

'He called me an angel,' Gwendal went on. 'Not as if it was a name for someone good or beautiful, but more like I was special . . . or unnatural.'

'Gwendal.' Milo gave him a hug. 'You're not unnatural, but you are special. Special to me and Mum.' And then, looking round at us. 'You're all special, and don't you forget it. We love you all.'

'Even Snow,' Andy swung his rat across the table.

'Not Snow,' said Milo.

Mum wasn't happy when she heard about Nathan Culfire and the bird. 'You'd better not go out unless one of us is with you, Dad or me,' she said when we were alone.

I thought this was over-reacting and said so.

'I know you can take care of yourself, Laura,' Mum said. 'It's Gwendal I'm worried about. He's at risk from . . . strangers and . . . unusual occurrences.'

I pondered this and came to the conclusion that

perhaps we were all at risk, now that Gwendal was living in our midst.

That night I couldn't bring myself to close my bedroom door. I needed the reassurance of Milo and Mary's late night chatter, their busy movements, their occasional laughter. But there was no laughter. A long, grave con-versation took place in the kitchen below my room, and then the lights went out before I had even been aware of their footsteps on the stairs, or the closing of their bedroom door. I did hear another door close, though. The front door.

I sat up, now wide awake. Mary and Milo hadn't come to bed. Why had they turned out the lights? Who had left the house?

I swung my feet out of bed and ran to the window. On the other side of the road a tall man stood looking up at the house. He wore a grey fedora.

I began to close the curtains tight against Nathan Culfire's stare, but a movement in the garden below caused me to leave a peep-hole, just wide enough for a view of Culfire and another man. My father.

Milo walked up to Culfire. He spoke to him, spreading his hands as though entreating him. Culfire towered above Milo, the shadows on his face moving ceaselessly. His reply seemed to have a dreadful urgency.

Milo took several steps backward. He looked shocked and angry. He shook his head.

Mr Culfire suddenly whipped round and strode away. For a moment Milo stood watching him, as though to make sure the man was leaving. Then, hands in his pockets, he stepped into the road.

What happened next I barely had time to understand. A shadow swept like lightning across my narrow view of the street. When it had gone Dad was lying in the gutter, and Mum was screaming.

4
A visit from the angel hunter

I ran downstairs and followed Mum into the street. But Milo was already getting to his feet, swearing horribly. I'd never been so happy to hear him swear.

'Damn cyclist,' he muttered. 'No lights. No bell. You'd think he was trying to hit me. God, my knees.'

Was it a cyclist? To me the flying shadow had looked too compact, too dark, and it had swept by so quietly.

'Did you see it, Mary?' Milo asked as he hobbled into the house.

'I saw you fall. I don't know, it could have been anything,' Mum said.

I took Dad's hand and heard myself say, 'It was supernatural. A horrible thing.'

He laughed. 'You saw it all, did you?'

'Yes, and Mr Culfire standing there, watching the house.'

Dad gave me a quick, nervous glance. 'Ah, Mr Culfire. We haven't seen the last of him, I'm afraid.'

Andy met us in the kitchen, complaining that Mum's scream had penetrated his earphones.

'You were intending to go to sleep eventually were you, Andy?' Dad remarked. 'It *is* one o'clock.'

Andy ignored this. 'What's going on?' he asked.

I tried to explain but Andy wasn't having any of the supernatural wolf stuff. He preferred straightforward crime, something that could be realistically tackled.

'If you'd seen Mr Culfire you'd believe in the supernatural,' I declared.

'He'll probably get that chance tomorrow,' Milo said.

'Why?' I cried. 'You're not going to let him into the house? How can you, Dad? Gwendal's really scared of him.'

Milo sighed. 'I don't think I can stop him, Laura.' He glanced at Mum. 'I only got rid of him by promising he could visit us tomorrow. I daresay he won't stay long.'

After what happened, why would Dad allow Nathan Culfire into our house? It obviously had something to do with Gwendal. The secrets were growing deeper and darker. On my way to bed I paused outside Gwendal's door. I thought the commotion might have woken him. From inside the room there came a series of clicks, almost like a tune. It was oddly soothing. Isidore was very much on guard tonight, I thought.

Milo didn't prepare for Culfire's visit. Perhaps he didn't realize that his house, his family and his very existence were under scrutiny.

Sundays were always a comfortable mess. When the doorbell rang, newspapers were strewn across the kitchen table and the cloth was covered in crumbs. Odd shoes and socks littered the hall. The sink was piled with dirty crockery and Lancelot was chewing a carrot under a chair.

Dad had tried to raid the swear box Polly made for him, and Mum was in the shower.

Andy, still in pyjamas and eating a banana, opened the door. Snow was enjoying a crust in his top pocket. I came up behind Andy, a second line of defence.

'Hi!' said Andy through a mouthful of banana.

Mr Culfire was only momentarily disconcerted. 'I've brought the bird,' he said, 'for . . . I suppose it must be your sister.' He held up a small cardboard box, its lid punctured by a pattern of airholes.

'Thanks!' Andy made to take the box.

Mr Culfire swung it out of his reach. 'I'd like to come in,' he said. 'I'm expected.'

'OK.' Andy opened the door a fraction wider and Mr Culfire strode into the hall. Picking his way between footwear he made for the kitchen. Milo just had time to shove his shirt-tail into his trousers.

Mr Culfire gave Milo a look of disapproval and then addressed the air above his head.

'Good morning, Mr McCool. I've brought the bird as promised.'

'Thank you!' Milo lifted his bandaged knuckles.

'You've had an accident,' Mr Culfire observed, making no attempt to hand over the box. A faint coo came from inside.

Dad shrugged. 'An aggressive cyclist, last night, just after you left as it happens.'

'So unfortunate.' Mr Culfire grimaced. 'The accident might not have happened, had you invited me in.'

'After midnight?' Milo's eyebrows lifted. 'This is a better time I think. Anyway, it was hardly an accident.'

'It might have been worse.' Our visitor's tone carried a hint of malice. Could it have been a warning? He seemed to have difficulty in selecting a chair; most of them were occupied by towels, toys and books. Andy and I watched his predicament with interest and it was Dad who eventually swept an armful of books on to the table.

'You do a great deal of reading, Mr McCool,' Mr Culfire remarked, taking the emptied chair.

'Don't we all,' said Milo, glancing at Andy. His sarcasm passed right over Andy's head because the poor bird was now making a frantic fluttering noise.

'I'll get Polly,' I said. 'I expect she'd like to take the pigeon outside.'

'Do that,' said Mr Culfire.

When I came back with Polly, Nathan Culfire turned expectantly. 'And the boy?' he demanded. 'Where's the boy?'

'He's not interested,' said Polly, snatching up the box. 'Is this the bird? How's its wing?'

'It wasn't broken,' Mr Culfire told her. 'They get exhausted, you know. It merely needed a rest. He's all yours, dear.'

'Thank you!' Polly hurried out with the box. She called, 'Are you coming, Laura, to see it fly?'

Andy followed Polly, but I stayed where I was. Instinct told me that Dad should not be left alone with Mr Culfire. There was a wolfish air about our visitor that seemed to put Milo's careless attitude at a definite disadvantage. I wished Dad had made more of an effort with his appearance. He really was a mess. Several buttons were undone, there was a stain on his sleeve and he hadn't shaved.

I watched Dad make a pot of strong coffee, five spoonfuls instead of four, and I waited for the wolf to make his move. Mr Culfire didn't like my nervous hovering, I could tell, but he didn't mention it. And I wasn't going to leave.

When the coffee was poured, Dad and I perched ourselves side by side on overloaded chairs, and Culfire said, 'You might not want a child to hear this.'

I gave Milo a desperate look of entreaty.

'I can't think what you would want to say to me, that Laura shouldn't hear,' Milo said in a tense voice.

'Indeed?' said Mr Culfire. 'Perhaps it's time they all knew the truth about their so-called brother.'

Dad's anxious face now wore a threatened look. 'Who are you? Where have you come from?'

'I'm from the Society for Angels.' The man's tone chilled me right through to my spine. 'And I've come to claim one of our own.' He lifted a hand as Milo made to stand up. 'Please, Mr McCool, hear me out. We were formed to protect the angels, to nurture them as it were, in a pure environment. You know what an angel is, dear?' He looked at me.

'They have wings,' I said.

He smiled indulgently. 'They were conceived in innocence.'

I was trying to work out what he meant, when he suddenly barked at Milo, 'Look at you! Look at this place! It's filthy. D'you really think you're the right father for an angel?' He glared at the swear box.

I hated the way he said that about Dad and our house.

'Angels are dead people,' I said angrily. 'Gwendal's just a boy. He's just our brother.'

'Come now, dear. You know very well he's not,' said Nathan Culfire.

I fell silent, waiting for someone to tell me about Gwendal's secret past.

Folding his arms across his chest, Mr Culfire settled back with a look of satisfaction. 'You haven't told your children the truth, have you, Mr McCool?' He didn't know about Dad's terrible talent for stories of course. 'A perfect opportunity for a lesson in eugenics, I should have thought. But, of course, you're afraid they would tell. And you can't afford to let that happen, can you? You've broken the law, Mr McCool, knowingly stepped into forbidden territory, and you can never go back, can you?'

Milo gave me an uneasy glance. It frightened me to see him look so trapped and helpless. What secret enterprise had brought him into this horrible situation, I couldn't begin to imagine.

As if the bite he'd taken out of Milo had not been large enough, the wolf began to gnaw deeper. This time he leaned close to his victim and I could smell the garlic on his breath. Not a vampire then, I thought, but it was hardly a relief. There were worse than vampires abroad.

'You're a failure, Mr McCool. A very sad failure, if you will allow me to say.'

Milo allowed it. I couldn't.

'Dad's not a failure,' I cried. 'He was famous once. He could do things you'd never manage, even in your wildest dreams. He . . .'

'*Once*,' said Mr Culfire 'Past tense.'

51

'He still could,' I protested.

'Laura!' Milo's firm hand closed over mine. 'Mr Culfire has more to say.'

'You mustn't let him,' I implored.

But Mr Culfire's opinions held a terrible fascination for Milo. It seemed that he had to hear them.

'We can't allow it, you know,' Mr Culfire said solemnly. 'To put it plainly, Mr McCool, you are a mess. You have recklessly ruined your body which leads me to believe you have also wrecked your brain. You seldom work . . . Oh, I know, you are a house-father,' he sneered. 'A house-father?'

'The best,' I said.

'Do me a favour, dear,' said Mr Culfire. 'I know what goes on here. Your clothes are infrequently washed, mostly unpressed. Your house is unclean and unsafe,' he glanced at Lancelot. 'Your meals are irregular and not particularly nourishing. It's Sunday, for goodness' sake, but where's the roast?'

'Actually,' said Milo, 'It's in the oven.'

'I can smell it,' Mum said from the doorway.

Mum's appearance drew a sigh of relief from Dad. 'Mary, this is our would-be midnight visitor. Mr Culfire, my wife.'

At that moment Polly rapped on the kitchen window. 'Look!' she called. The pigeon was perched on her out-stretched wrist. 'He won't go,' she sang. 'He keeps coming back. I can even dance with him.' This she proceeded to do.

The small swaying figure, observed through a mist of net curtain, lifted me out of the darkness that Culfire had brought into our house. I felt Dad's spirits rise too, though he had a long way to go before he was his old carefree self again. Nevertheless he had the strength to walk away from our visitor and say, 'We've heard enough, Mr Culfire. It would be a good idea if you left now.'

'I must see the boy,' Culfire protested.

'No!' Milo swung round, his green eyes dangerous. 'You must *not*!' he shouted.

Mum looked enquiringly at me, but I couldn't enlighten her just then.

Andy and Snow drifted onto the scene. Andy looked even more like one of the lost boys, his pyjamas having acquired brown knees after a romp in the garden.

'Another rodent!' Culfire proclaimed. It wasn't clear whether he was referring to Andy or his rat.

'I think my husband asked you to leave,' Mary said. Her icy tone was somehow more dramatic than Milo's shouting.

Mr Culfire made a strange bow in her direction and then, addressing Milo, he said, 'I'll give you a week. Time for you to prepare our boy – our angel.'

'If you mean Gwendal, he's not your boy,' said Mum. 'He's ours.'

'I don't think he is, my dear,' Nathan Culfire said spitefully. 'And I suggest you tell at least two of your children exactly what he is. It's rather unfair, don't you think, to keep them in the dark. One day the whole world will know.'

'Over my dead body,' Milo said.

'So be it!' Mr Culfire picked up his stoat-grey hat and fitting it over his head, made a sudden dart to the door. As he passed me I could smell his clothes, which must have been of a great age, because I began to feel quite dizzy. Or was it his softly spoken threat, 'So be it!'

No one saw him out. The front door slammed and a silence fell, until Andy said, 'Wee-irrd!' Something of an understatement, I thought.

The pale-winged pigeon fluttered across the window behind Dad and settled on a branch. 'Good-bye!' Polly's voice sang out from somewhere. But the pigeon didn't seem inclined to move further than our garden.

'Tell us about Gwendal,' Andy said.

'Not now, Andy!' Mum looked at Dad.

'You have to,' I said fiercely, and then I saw why they couldn't. Gwendal was staring at us from the doorway. Isidore was clutched to his chest.

'Hey, what's that?' said Andy.

Gwendal had kept his secret very well. I was the only one to have seen the robot. Now Gwendal came forward and stood Isidore on the table. The little robot clicked and sighed and turned a full circle. When it came to rest, Gwendal said, 'Isidore can help.'

Mum and Dad looked surprised. Mum put her arm round Gwendal and asked, 'But what is it, Gwendal? What is Isidore?'

'It's a robot,' Andy said impatiently. 'It's brilliant! Where did it come from, Gwendal?'

'I made it,' Gwendal said.

Andy looked at him. 'Really?'

'He did,' I said.

Milo leaned across the table. 'What d'you mean, it can help?' he asked Gwendal.

'Isidore's my friend,' Gwendal told him. 'He can listen, spy on people. He can send messages to . . . well, if that man wants to take me back . . .'

'He's not from the clinic, Gwendal,' Milo said. 'Mr Culfire is from some secret society or other. Perhaps because you're different . . . gifted he wants to take you away from us. From me at any rate. He seems to think that, as a father, I'm pretty inadequate.'

'You're not! You're not!' cried Gwendal emphatically. 'Please don't say I'm different. I'm no different to hundreds of boys. I'm just . . . just me. Perhaps if he found another gifted boy he'd leave us alone and take him.'

Milo could lie beautifully, but he couldn't hide his deepest feelings, his face was too generous for that. I didn't understand his expression just then. He'd never looked so grave, so grimly determined. 'No one's going to take you from us, Gwendal,' he said quietly.

Gwendal smiled and picked up Isidore. 'Come and see what he can do,' he said to Andy.

'Right.' Andy, beaming, followed Gwendal out of the kitchen, while Mum yelled at him to put some clothes on.

That afternoon there was a break in the drizzly day. The sun came out and swept Polly's creamy bird into the sky and far away. Polly pretended to be glad for it, but then she began to pine. So Andy let her take Flake and the seven ratlets into her bedroom for the night.

After supper Andy and I watched a movie on television. It went on for hours, a real saga, and by the time it was over Polly and Gwendal were in bed and asleep.

Andy turned off the TV and we were just about to go upstairs when Mum and Dad came into the sitting-room.

They looked apprehensive and when I went to kiss them goodnight, Dad said, 'Wait a minute, Laura. We want to talk to you.'

I stepped back, afraid of his solemn face.

'It's all right,' Mum said, almost in a whisper. 'It's nothing serious, well, it is serious, but nothing worrying.'

Andy dropped down on to the sofa and I sat beside him. Milo and Mary took armchairs either side of us. Dad swivelled round so that he was looking directly at us, and I felt a weight of trouble and foreboding.

'Please, don't look so stricken, Laura,' Dad begged me. 'It's nothing that can hurt you. It's not a problem. It's just something that we feel you two should know. But we have to trust you never to tell a soul.'

'We won't.' Andy spoke for both of us. I felt as though a rock had been dropped deep into my stomach. I didn't want to know their secret if it brought so much uneasiness into their faces.

'It's about Gwendal, isn't it?' said Andy.

'Yes,' Milo replied.

'We know he's not our brother,' I said. 'We guessed that anyway.'

'Ssh!' Milo put a finger to his lips. 'We don't want to wake them, Polly and Gwendal.' He took a breath. 'No one in the history of the world has ever had to do this.'

We didn't say, 'do what?' though I knew it was on Andy's mind as well as mine.

'I'll tell you how it happened,' said Mum. She always went straight to the point and in many ways she was easier to understand than Milo. But she left out the little details that coloured events and made them into stories.

'As you know,' she began, 'Milo was a very active actor. He was often badly injured. When you were six months old, Laura, Dad had the worst of his accidents. He was in hospital for two months. I was frantic. We had no health insurance, no savings, no income and nowhere to live. I was staying with your grandmother, not the easiest of people to get on with. She only had two bedrooms.'

Even without the details Mum painted a pretty grim picture. Every day she would visit Dad in hospital, and sometimes she'd take us with her – Andy toddling, me in her arms, and every time she left she'd have tears in her eyes, wondering if Dad would ever walk again, and even if he did, how we would all manage to survive. And then, one day, as she was leaving hospital in this very sorry state, she met a man who opened a window and gave her a view of a bright and shining future.

'It meant breaking the law,' Milo said, 'and when your mum told me I didn't want her to go through with it, but I was in no fit state to argue. And so I let it happen. And I've never regretted it.'

So something had happened to Mum in those shadowy years before Polly was born. But what did it have to do with Gwendal?

5
The truth about Gwendal

I've never excelled at biology. In fact you could definitely place me towards the bottom of the class in that area. I can't remember where all the tubes, the ventricles and arteries go, and I always confuse the organs (offal as Milo puts it), the liver, lungs and kidneys. As far as the heart goes, I've been more influenced by a painting I once saw than by anything our biology teacher told us. It was a picture of Jesus with this lovely sparkling heart right in the middle of his chest. I'm told that this is not its exact location, but that's where I put it, because I like to think of it there, plumb in the middle, radiating goodness.

The subject that occupied the four of us for the next half-hour was biology, or to be more specific, genetics. So I had to cling very hard to everything that was said.

Andy came straight out and asked what Mum had had to do in order to achieve this bright and shining future. 'Is this it?' he asked, waving his arm round our dusty, cluttered living-room. 'Is this the brilliant future you were offered?'

'Yes,' said Mary sternly. 'And if you had no home and

no means of getting one, you'd find this house paradise. It cost a great deal of money.'

Andy was silent. I wanted them to get back to Gwendal, to what happened to Mum and how they had broken the law. 'Who was this man?' I asked. 'And what did he want you to do?'

'He asked me to have a baby.'

'A baby?' It seemed so simple. 'You mean he wanted you to have his baby because his wife couldn't have any?' I didn't like the idea, but I knew it wasn't breaking the law.

'No,' Mum said. 'Not that.'

'Donor sperm?' Andy offered. 'I saw it on TV. It was the other way round. A man couldn't have children, so his wife was given another man's baby. Was it a sort of experiment?'

'Milo can have children,' Mum looked at Dad. 'He's had three of you, remember!'

'Three?' I said. 'Not Gwendal, then?'

Dad still wasn't ready to admit this. 'The man that Mary met had nothing to do with the baby,' he said. 'He was an agent for someone else. Someone very rich who, we were told, could never have children of his own. This state of affairs preyed on his mind. He felt he had so much to give a child, so much to pass on, not only his great wealth but also, presumably, his own intellect, his wisdom.'

Milo gave a wry smile. 'Some scientists and doctors are not too fastidious about the law. To be given unlimited funds that enable them to extend the boundaries of science, this was enough of an incentive. They didn't even want fame, all they wanted was to satisfy their curiosity.

So our rich man had no difficulty in finding the team he wanted.'

'To do what?' said Andy. 'It seems like he wanted a magician rather than a doctor.'

'To make a baby out of gingerbread,' I said, trying to lighten the atmosphere. 'But it still wouldn't be him, would it, it wouldn't have his genes. And that's what he wanted, another version of himself.'

'Exactly,' said Milo. 'He wanted to replicate himself.'

I saw the word 'replicate' as though it were a picture brightly lit, and I made a sudden guess, 'A clone,' I said. 'He wanted to clone himself.'

'Yes,' said Milo. 'And to give birth to his clone he needed a mother. A woman desperate enough to break the law, a healthy woman who was wise enough to keep silent, and clever enough to appreciate the child should he wish to live with her.'

'Mums like that don't grow on trees,' Andy observed, and we both looked at our mother who fitted the bill perfectly.

'How did they do it?' I ventured. 'How did they make a clone?'

Andy knew the answer: 'They suck the nucleus out of a female's egg, all the genetic material, the DNA and stuff, so that it's empty, and then they put in a cell from another animal, and they give it a shot of electricity to tell the egg it's fertilized and Bingo: the female gives birth to something that doesn't have her genes or anything to do with her. They did it to a sheep and a clone called Dolly was born. They've done it with mice too. They've even put human genes into cows and pigs.'

Andy was talking about animals. We were talking about Gwendal, and it seemed wrong, somehow, that we should be discussing him as if he were just a cluster of genes. 'Gwendal's a boy,' I said, 'not a monster, not just an experiment.'

'Gwendal?' It hadn't dawned on Andy. His interest in animals had diverted him from the subject of our discussion 'But a human being has never been cloned,' he said. 'It would die.'

Strange and impossible as it seemed, one hadn't died.

Mary and Milo stared at us, helplessly. I suppose they were willing us to understand and support what they had done. But I could only think of Gwendal and how I might feel if I were him. Where would you belong? Where would you fit? I understood now the great emptiness that appeared to follow him on that very first day, and I began to feel frightened, not only for him, but for all of us. It was like living somewhere where nobody knew you.

'So who is this rich man?' I asked.

Milo had difficulty in answering this. 'I don't know,' he said at last. 'I tried to find out, but it was never possible. At the clinic he is always referred to as the "Sponsor". He sent a list of names, that's all, and Mary chose the name Gwendal. She can't explain why.'

Was it my imagination, or did I hear the tiniest creak outside the door? Milo looked towards it, frowning, but he didn't move.

'So somewhere in the world there's another Gwendal,' I said quietly. 'But Gwendal doesn't know, does he? He doesn't even know what he is.'

Mary murmured, 'It seems that no one has told him.

So how can we?'

'Can you help us?' Milo asked Andy and me. 'Do you think he should know?'

Andy said, 'Yes,' but I wasn't sure that was the right answer. I felt so tired I couldn't put my mind to such an enormous question. 'I don't know,' I said dully. I stood up, longing to lay my head on a pillow and not think about how Gwendal's existence had changed our lives.

Milo caught hold of my hand. 'Laura, we can trust you not to tell anyone about this, can't we?'

'I wouldn't know *how* to tell anyone.' I kissed Mum and Dad and opened the sitting room door. Almost simultaneously there was a soft click above me and I thought, he knows. He's heard everything, and if I can't sleep because of what I've heard, how can he?'

In the morning I knew what I had suspected. Gwendal had been outside that door. Without a doubt he had heard what was said.

When I left for school, I tried to sound casual. 'Bye then, Gwendal,' I said, but he didn't look up. He stared doggedly at his bowl of cornflakes and I could see the space around him widening. The emptiness stole out towards me until I could feel the edge of it creep across my fingertips, and I did something I could never forgive myself for. I ran away from it.

I grabbed my bag, tore open the door and ran, while Andy called, 'Hey! Hold on, Laura. What's bitten you?'

Andy pounded after me but I kept on running until we were almost at the school gates. Then I slowed down and said breathlessly, 'He knows.'

'So what,' said Andy. 'He's not going to blab, is he?'

'That's not the point,' Andy's attitude shocked me. 'Imagine how he must feel.'

'I can't.' Andy didn't look at me as he marched towards the gates. 'That's just it. I can't imagine. And I'm not sure I believe. I've read all about cl . . . about them. It took hundreds of attempts to make Dolly, and it's never happened with a human being . . . never.'

'But why should Mum and Dad lie?' I said, 'and how d'you think we got the house?'

'I don't know.' Andy forged ahead. He'd seen his friend, Gary Allen, with a football. 'But I wouldn't put anything past Milo, would you?'

Would I? Did I really know what Dad was capable of? I knew I could trust him and that seemed to be all that mattered.

During break I went to the library to surf the internet for stuff about clones. I learnt quite a lot. The school librarian, Miss Baker, moves very quietly, and I wasn't aware that she was reading over my shoulder until a voice close to my ear, said, 'Clones, Laura? Is this a sudden interest?'

She gave me such a fright I jumped in my seat. My cheeks burned and I couldn't answer her.

'It's all right,' she said, with some surprise. 'There's nothing illicit there. It's rather an intriguing subject as a matter of fact.'

I was afraid I had given our secret away, and then I realized that anyone could have an interest in cloning, it wasn't necessary to have one in the family. I logged out of the computer and told her I'd got the information I needed.

When school was over I found that I wasn't looking forward to an evening at home. I usually ran the last few yards, but today my feet dragged, my bag felt heavier than usual and my head ached.

Andy and Polly were already tucking in when I walked into the kitchen. Gwendal wasn't there. I asked where he was. Dad said, 'Nibbled a biscuit and went upstairs again. He's working on something with his . . . with Isidore. Been at it all day.'

I wanted to ask if Gwendal had given any sign that he'd heard our night-time conversation, but I couldn't with Polly sitting there – ears as sharp as Lancelot's.

After tea I tried to do some homework, but I couldn't concentrate. I kept seeing Gwendal's small head bent over his cornflakes. I had to know if he'd heard us.

I found him sitting at his computer. He was con-cen-trating fiercely on his work, but he smiled when I came in, so he was pleased to see me.

There was a large black box on his bed and, lying beside it, a strange silvery suit, like a mini space-suit.

'What's this, then?' I picked up a leg of the suit.

'Virtual reality,' he murmured.

'Wow! Can I . . .'

'No,' he said. 'Not now.' His eyes never left the monitor. 'Sorry, Laura, am I being selfish?'

'I feel the same about some of my possessions,' I admitted.

Isidore stood erect beside the keyboard and I noticed that a cable from the computer had been attached to his back. He was unusually quiet.

'What are you working on, Gwendal?' I sat behind

him and watched a succession of maps flip across the screen. Then we were on to deserts, fields, jungles, oceans, mountains and forests. As the cursor swam across the world I realized that Gwendal was engaged in a search.

'What are you looking for?'

'He's cleverer than I am,' Gwendal murmured.

'Who?'

'My sponsor. He's made it like a game.'

'You heard us last night. Did you hear every word?'

'Families are no good at secrets are they?' An icy little sentence that told me everything.

'Are you . . . does it worry you?'

'I've been too busy trying to find out who I am.' Still he kept his eyes on the screen.

'You're you, Gwendal. You still belong with us, you know. I looked it up. Mary is your legal parent. That's good, isn't it?'

'I suppose.' He tore his eyes from the screen for a second, and I saw how pale he was, how huge his sleepless blue eyes. 'But you know what I mean. I must find *him*, the one who I am.'

I knew how frightened he must be to find out what he was. 'Have you told Dad?' I asked.

'Told him?'

'Told him that you heard us. That you know.'

He froze for a moment, then slowly shook his head. 'NO.'

'You should,' I said.

'No.' Again he shook his head. 'And you mustn't tell them.'

'Why?' I wanted him to share his fear with Mum and Dad. I didn't think I could cope with it alone.

'No,' he said fiercely. 'I've always known something was wrong with me, that I was different. I just didn't know what it was. Don't tell them that I heard. Not yet.'

I understood then, that telling would be like admitting it was true, and Gwendal couldn't face that yet. The shock of finding out must have been very great. He needed a breathing space. It was like Milo lying about Gran when she died, because he needed time to come to terms with the truth.

'Promise,' he said again. 'Not yet.'

'I promise I won't tell them that you know, until you're ready. Do you want me to help you with that?' I nodded at the screen.

'No. I've got Isidore. He's full of information. I'll show you when we've cracked it.'

'OK.' Reluctantly, I left him to get on with his search.

We didn't see much of Gwendal during the next three days. He emerged for meals, looking pale and tense, and spoke hardly a word. Dad kept trying to draw him into our conversations, and cooking his favourite meals. But Gwendal ate less and less. He would push his food around the plate until it got cold, and then leave the table.

I longed to tell Dad the truth, but I couldn't break my promise to Gwendal.

Andy was becoming a problem, too, and Andy had never been a problem before. He'd always been the one to see the funniest side of a situation. Not this situation, though. He couldn't bear Dad's preoccupation with

Gwendal, and snapped at me whenever I tried to defend them.

Polly spent a great deal of time with Mum when she was home. She could hardly wait for her to come in. They would discuss Polly's day, Polly's friends. They would dance to the latest pop song and chatter on about food and fashion.

I could feel our family cracking apart and I didn't know how to stop it. I thought that Milo was too concerned with Gwendal to notice, but I discovered that he had other problems on his mind. He had taken Mr Culfire's threat seriously.

When I stepped through the front door on Friday, I found the house so changed I barely recognized it. Every wooden surface gleamed with polish, stains had been lifted from carpets, windows sparkled, wellies stood shoulder to shoulder in the porch. Clothes hung on hooks, shoes were nowhere to be seen. As for the kitchen – I had never beheld such shining tiles, such a gleaming empti-ness. The smell left a lot to be desired but I daresay disinfectants have to be chosen by people with a nose for these things. Milo never had much of a sense of smell. In the midst of this gleam and glitter, he sat exhausted at the kitchen table.

'What d'you think?' he said, as Andy and I stepped into his bright new territory.

'What happened?' I said.

'I've been cleaning,' he told us.

'Why?' Andy dumped his bag by the door.

'It gives us a better chance with Mr Culfire,' Milo explained. 'When he sees our neat clean house, perhaps he'll consider me worthy enough to care for an angel.'

'Hunh!' Andy muttered.

Nothing had been done about tea, so I put the kettle on and began to lay the table. 'You don't think he was serious, do you?' I said. 'I mean he can't take Gwendal away from us. The person who gives birth to a clone is its legal mother. Did you know that?'

'I did as a matter of fact,' Dad said. 'But as the whole situation is illegal in this country, I can't see that it makes a difference.'

Andy hauled his bag up again and made for the door. 'Let me know when tea's ready. If there's going to *be* any tea.'

Milo watched him go with a solemn face.

'Don't mind Andy,' I said. 'He's just in a mood.' I made two cups of tea and brought them to the table.

'What would I do without you?' Dad said.

I sat beside him and he took my hand. 'Gwendal doesn't exist, Lo,' he said. 'At least not on paper, not in a record. And if ever it came to light, well, I just can't imagine what would happen. He may well be taken from us.'

It made me cold to hear Dad repeat Gwendal's words. 'He said that,' I murmured. 'He told us he didn't exist.'

'Lo, d'you think he knows?'

I looked into Dad's changeable eyes and I wanted to tell him the truth. It hurt so much to lie, but I couldn't break faith with Gwendal, so I said the only thing I could, 'I don't know.'

Milo gave a huge sigh.

'I don't understand why Culfire wants him,' I said.

'This stuff about Gwendal being an angel, what does it mean?'

Milo tried to explain. He told me there was a group of people, once, who believed that if ever a clone were born, it would be a sort of angel. Other children were conceived when their parents had sex. They were conceived during a physical act, whereas a clone would be 'conceived' in a laboratory – in innocence. It would have no parents. It would be untouched by sin, as Dad put it. We've always been very frank in our house. I'd known about birth and conception since I was Polly's age, but this sounded so difficult, so clinical. How could it have anything to do with angels?

'D'you remember the little prince – how he appeared in the desert, and then disappeared?' I said. 'I suppose he was a sort of angel.'

Dad smiled. 'We won't let Gwendal disappear,' he said.

'It sounds so sad,' I went on. 'Even an orphan had parents once. Even people who are adopted or fostered had them. But not to have had any . . . ever . . .'

'I do have parents.' The voice came from the hall, a small, chilly voice. Gwendal appeared in the doorway.

'Gwendal!' Dad half-rose from the table, then sat down again.

Gwendal came into the room but stood where he couldn't be touched. 'I've found him,' he said.

'Him?' Dad looked anxious.

'Him who I am,' said Gwendal. 'I don't know what else to call him.'

Milo slouched in his chair with a helpless smile. 'Gwendal, we are your parents,' he said.

'No,' said Gwendal. *They* are. He has shown me. Come and see.'

We followed him upstairs, Dad wearing a frown, me burning with curiosity. In the wonderfully tidy room, Isidore was standing to attention beside the computer. He seemed to be regarding us with an earnest expression, though I can't say his features had been rearranged in any way.

Gwendal chose me to be the first to see what he had found. From the black box that now sat on the floor, he took the silver suit and a gleaming helmet. The crown and earflaps were a shiny silver, and the mask that covered half the face was the smoky blue-black of bird feathers. Gwendal attached a cable from Isidore to the back of this impressive head-set, saying. 'Put the suit on first.'

I obediently took off my shoes and began to pull the suit up, beginning at my feet. It was a tight fit but I just about managed to squeeze into it.

When he was satisfied that I was properly zipped up, Gwendal fitted the helmet over my head.

At first I was plunged into such silent darkness I began to feel I was floating in space, and then I heard a sound I recognized. The wash of water on sand, the splash of a tumbling wave. I covered the headphones with my hands, the sounds were so real, and then I found that I was walking by the sea. I could almost feel the wet sand under my feet.

In the distance two figures were approaching. As they walked across the shining stretch of sand between us, the wind blew in from the sea, and I felt the spray that brushed their faces as though it were touching my own.

They drew nearer and I saw that they were holding hands. The woman was small with very delicate features. She wore a white dress sprigged with blue flowers, and her hair, which had been pinned to the top of her head, had escaped in the wind in long flying tendrils. She was carrying a stiff straw hat with a black ribbon round the crown.

The man was also carrying his hat, a soft brown colour with a wide brim. He wore a light brown suit, the jacket belted at the waist. I found that I was moving towards them, my footsteps splashing though the edge of the surf.

As I reached their clasped hands they smiled and looked at me with great tenderness, or were they looking at each other, because I was passing between them now. They spoke very softly but I heard two words. She said, 'Jean,' and he said, 'Véronique.' His eyes were very dark and hers were as blue as the sky. I was beyond them now, and when I looked back they were disappearing round the curve of a wooded cliff.

The headset was lifted away from me and I found myself sitting on Gwendal's bed again, with Milo beside me. It took me several seconds to adjust to the cold colour in the room. I had been walking through such a soft evening light.

Gwendal smiled triumphantly. 'You see,' he said.

'How d'you know who they are?' I asked.

'I told my sponsor to send me something of my parents. I just wanted to be sure. Specially my mother. She's pretty isn't she? He wouldn't send a picture of himself. I have to go and see him, he says.'

Milo frowned at that.

'He made the programme out of old photographs and sounds of the sea. He is so clever. So it is them, you see.' Gwendal looked happier than he had for days.

'But you still don't know who he is?' I said.

'I don't have the whole name, yet. And I'm not sure where lives. But I've reached him, you see. Dr Mac at the clinic gave me a code. He said I could use it if I needed to. I thought I never would.'

We both understood why he had needed to use the code.

'Don't worry, Milo,' Gwendal said quietly. 'I was bound to find out sometime. I knew I was different. I didn't like the idea, once, but I can – get used to it.' It was the first time I had heard him use Milo's name, instead of calling him Dad.

Milo didn't want to wear the silver helmet. He shook his head when Gwendal offered it to him. 'Another time,' he said and left the room looking tired and troubled.

'He's been cleaning all day,' I told Gwendal. 'So that when Culfire comes the place will look clean enough for an angel.'

'Don't say that,' Gwendal muttered. 'I'm not an angel.'

'OK.' I stood up and patted Isidore's head. 'Isidore did well. I presume he helped to bring your parents here.'

'Of course. Did you like them, Laura?'

How could one like two figures from another age? 'They were . . . beautiful,' I said, and then a sudden thought struck me. The couple in Gwendal's programme would be very old by now. In fact they could even be dead, but I couldn't bring myself to mention this.

Downstairs I found Andy frying himself an egg. 'I wish

Mum would come home,' he said. 'I'm starving. Dad seems to be out of it today.'

I told him about the headset and Gwendal's parents.

'Weird,' he said. 'The whole thing's weird. Why doesn't he just go away?'

'Where would he go?'

'Back to where he came from.' Andy scraped his egg on to a slice of toast. 'He's just a load of trouble.'

'Don't ever let me hear you say that again!' Milo came in from the hall, carrying a bucket and mop.

'OK, Mrs Mop,' Andy said flippantly.

Milo banged his bucket down on to the tiles. I couldn't imagine what would have happened next if Mum hadn't arrived with bags of delicious food hanging from her arms.

'Milo, you're a genius,' she cried. 'It looks like a palace.'

Thanks to Mum the evening wasn't as bad as it might have been, which was just as well, because we needed all our strength for the next day.

Our visitor didn't arrive until the afternoon, by which time Andy had left for his football match, and Mum and Polly were out shopping for shoes. Gwendal shut himself safely in his room.

Milo paced the kitchen, checked the hall for litter, fretted over the orange peel he found in the living-room and locked Snow into his cage.

'How d'you know Mr Culfire will come,' I said. 'It might have been an empty threat.'

'It wasn't, believe me.' He showed me a card that he'd been carrying in his pocket. The Angel on the front had

73

folded pure white wings. It seemed to be praying. On the back of the card a cryptic message had been scrawled in spiderlike writing: 'Make sure he's ready.'

When the doorbell went I made myself brave enough to answer it. Nathan Culfire loomed on the step. He seemed to cast a shadow all the way to the back of the hall. Removing his grey fedora, he said coldly, 'Is he ready?'

'No he's not,' Milo came up behind me. 'Come in, Mr Culfire.'

Mr Culfire stepped inside. He appeared not to notice the immaculate tidiness, the scrubbed floor or the gleaming windowpanes. He wouldn't even enter our won-der-fully hygienic kitchen or glance into the neat living-room. He remained where he was, crowding our small hall with his age and hollowness – a black hole came to mind.

'Come and see our kitchen,' I invited. 'You wouldn't believe the miracle that's happened.'

'Don't speak of miracles,' he said. It sounded like a threat.

Milo said, 'I'll make a cup of tea and we can discuss our – problem.'

'There's nothing to discuss.' Mr Culfire didn't move. 'Where's the boy?'

'This is ridiculous. You know it is. You can't take a boy from his home.' Milo was beginning to lose his temper.

'You can't stop me, Mr McCool.'

'Look what Dad's done,' I said, 'All the cleaning, just to impress you.'

Milo shook his head and frowned at me.

'Too late, I'm afraid,' said Mr Culfire. 'Where is he? In his room?' He turned to the stairs.

Milo moved swiftly. Throwing out an arm he stepped in front of him. 'Leave our house,' he said.

Mr Culfire stopped and smiled. But he was hesitating. He was a thin, unhealthy man, his bones probably crisp and frail.

'Now.' Milo could look dangerous when he wanted. He might have broken many bones but he was still fit. Mr Culfire was obviously aware of this. He turned abruptly and walked to the front door. 'Have it your way, Mr McCool,' he said. 'You'll regret it.'

It was only when I felt Dad's arms round me that I realized I was shaking. 'Don't let him come back, Dad,' I whispered.

'I'll try, Laura.' Milo replied gently.

I knew that even if he did his very best it wouldn't be enough. Nathan Culfire would come back.

Gwendal had crept out of his room. 'Is it over?' he called down. 'Has he gone?'

'It's over for now,' Dad told him, and then he laughed. 'Silly old fool, who does he think he is?'

I laughed too, I was so glad to see the back of that skulking grey shape. Gwendal ran down the stairs with a big grin on his face. 'Safe. Safe!' he cried. 'For now.'

I wanted to open all the doors and windows and breathe fresh air. 'Let's go into the garden,' I said. Gwendal followed me, eager to cuddle Lancelot. It was already dusk, but the garden seemed safe and airy, with its ivy-covered walls and dewy grass. I thought that Mr Culfire would be far away by now. But, of course, it was more of a wish than a belief.

'I'm going to check the rope,' Milo said. 'I want to

75

make sure it's safe.' It was a rope that Andy used to swing, Tarzan-like, across the garden and back to the tree.

I watched Milo climb high into the tree, brushing the wind-chimes as he moved. The rope was attached to a long branch about six metres from the ground. As Milo stretched out to the top of the rope, the chimes pealed an eerie tune and I didn't hear the creak of the garden gate.

'Laura!' Milo called suddenly, his tone loud and fearful.

I turned and saw them stealing towards Gwendal, who was bent over the rabbit hutch. Two figures, grey and wolf-like.

'Gwendal!' I screamed. I reached for his hand and dragged him towards the house.

What did they expect, those wolves? Did they think Milo was too far away? That he'd stay safe in the tree while a child was stolen? That he'd never risk his life for someone who didn't belong anywhere?

When I looked back my father was falling through the air.

6

The wolves attack

He landed just behind one of them, pushing him to the ground. The creature gave a yelp and the other one shrank away, sliding through the dusk quiet as a ghost.

I clung to Gwendal's hand while Milo and the wolf fought together in the dead grass. Milo knew how to fall, he'd done it many times, but this jump had been from a very great height, and he was winded. The wolf was bound to win eventually. At last he shook Milo off and stood above him. I don't know what he was going to do then, but I found a howl coming from inside me and I rushed at him.

Perhaps he saw a bit of a beast in me, something he hadn't expected. Whatever it was he turned and ran. But before he spun away I looked into his face and saw that, of course, he wasn't a wolf at all, but a man with pale cold eyes.

I watched him tumble through the gate and out on to the path, then I turned back to Dad. Gwendal was kneeling beside him, not knowing what to do. Milo was holding his stomach but it was his face that looked a mess. 'Only a nose-bleed,' he said, grinning through the blood. 'My God, he got me in the gut, though.'

We helped him indoors but didn't have time to clean him up before Mum arrived. When she walked in there was blood all over Dad's face and shirt, and a dark bruise arriving on his jaw.

'What? What happened?' she cried.

'Fell out of the tree,' Dad lied quickly, his eyes turning mossy-green.

'There's so much blood!' Polly exclaimed.

'Noses bleed a lot,' Milo told her cheerfully. 'See, it's stopped now.'

Mum stared at him suspiciously, then she ran a tea-cloth under the cold water tap and began to dab at Milo's nose. 'Oh, Milo,' she said. 'This is becoming a very bad habit.'

Apart from an occasional grimace he seemed to be rather pleased with himself. A state that irritated Mum considerably. When Polly ran off to try on the new shoes, she asked, 'Did he come?'

'Yes,' said Milo, 'and he went away.'

'Is this the result of his visit?'

'Not precisely. I'll tell you later. Right now I'm going to change my shirt.'

Mum gave an exaggerated sigh and began to ring out the bloodied tea-towel in the sink. I put her shopping into cupboards. The kitchen looked so nice I wanted it to stay that way as long as possible. Gwendal stood watching us for a while. He looked scared and lonely and I wished Mum would pay him more attention, but her thoughts were all with Milo. Eventually Gwendal trailed off to his room.

When Andy came in I followed him upstairs and told him what had happened.

Andy didn't say anything. He took Snow out of his cage and let him run across the bed. Then he sat beside the rat and watched him clean himself.

'Maybe we should just let him go with Mr Culfire,' he said.

'We can't!' I shouted. 'He belongs here.'

'That's all you know. If the Society for Angels wants Gwendal so badly perhaps he'd be better off there. Pretty soon Culfire will blackmail Dad by threatening to leak the news to the press. Imagine the fuss there'd be – a human clone!'

'He can't do that,' I said angrily, 'because he can't prove it. He'd be laughed at.'

'Hm!' Andy picked up his rat and let him run up to his shoulder.

I had a sudden suspicion. 'Andy, you wouldn't tell anyone about Gwendal would you?'

'No. Like you said, who'd believe me. But I think Dad ought to have told the police about those kidnappers, or whatever they were.'

'He couldn't,' I said. 'They'd want to know everything. Who Gwendal was. Why it happened.'

'He's not going to tell Mum about the kidnappers either, is he?' Andy grumbled. 'This has become a house of secrets and I don't like it.'

I didn't like the way Andy seemed to be changing, but during the next few days I began to understand him. And he was right about the secrets. Mum was never told about what happened in the garden.

Dad wouldn't leave Gwendal alone in the house after the wolves' invasion, not for a second. So Andy and I had to walk Polly to school and fetch her afterwards. Jessica's mother was out of the question. Since the pirate episode Jessica and Polly hadn't spoken to each other. Andy and I had to take notes to school, so that we could leave early. On the third day Dad rang the primary school and arranged for someone to stay with Polly until we arrived.

Andy forgot to mention he had a football match after school. I had to fetch Polly alone. That's when the wolves decided to show their snouts again.

The primary school is in a very green part of the city. Rhododendron bushes crowd behind the walls and tall trees grow on both sides of the road. The clocks had just been put back and it was getting dark. Even the street lighting was hampered somehow by the long branches, and the pavement was murky and mysterious. I had almost reached the school when a dark form sailed towards me on rollerblades. He moved fast round the groups of pedestrians, his arms flying, but when he saw me the wolf folded his arms and rolled, his blades neatly placed together. I leapt to one side and as he passed he gave me one of his pale-eyed stares. Pressed against the wall I glanced back and found him looking at me over his shoulder.

I bounded away from the wall and ran all the way to the school, across the playground and up the steps, where I thumped on the glass-panelled door.

Mrs Dawes emerged and let me in. 'Are you all right, Laura?' she asked. 'You look worried.'

'I've been running,' I said. 'I'm in a bit of a hurry.'

'Where's Andy?'

'Football match,' I panted.

'How's the new school? Are you getting on OK?'

I like Mrs Dawes and normally I'd have spent more time talking to her but I wanted to get Polly home safely. I wanted to be safe myself. 'It's all right,' I said. 'We've got to go now, Mrs Dawes.' And I called, 'Polly! Polly!'

Polly ran out of a classroom and I grabbed her hand. But Mrs Dawes wasn't quite ready to let me go.

'How's the long-lost brother? It must be so good to have him home at last.'

'What?' My mouth hung open and I know I looked stupid. It was a shock to hear her mention Gwendal, but I remembered that Polly hadn't been sworn to silence. However, as far as Mrs Dawes knew, Gwendal was just an ordinary boy. I pulled myself together and said, 'Yes,' very abruptly. 'Goodbye, Mrs Dawes.'

Mrs Dawes let us out and locked the door behind us. I turned to wave but she had gone.

'We've got to run,' I told Polly. 'We'll go the back way.'

'Why? It's longer,' Polly complained.

'I want to get something at the shop.' I tugged her hand.

The back way led through a street of small shops. I thought we'd be safer there, where the streetlights were brighter and people were bustling about shopping.

As we came out of the school gates I looked to see if the wolf had gone. He was nowhere to be seen, but I still ran in the opposite direction.

When we reached the post office, I allowed a brief rest and then we walked past the shops. The windows looked so bright, the shoppers so ordinary and reliable, that the wolf seemed a creature of my imagination.

We turned a corner, and as we left the shops behind I felt as though we were stepping into a dangerous space.

'Run, now,' I said, tugging Polly's hand.

'Why've we got to run?' she moaned.

'Dad told me to,' I said, hoping he'd find a reason when we got home.

Polly usually runs or skips everywhere, but by the time we'd made a second turn, into our own street, she'd had enough. She had a stitch in her side and she kept fussing that her bag was too heavy.

'I'll carry your bag,' I said.

I was lifting it off her shoulders when I saw them. Just a movement out of the corner of my eye, but I knew they were there.

'Run, Polly!' I cried, heaving at her bag. 'You've got to run as fast as you can.'

'Why?' she whimpered. Somehow half her jacket had come away with the strap of her bag and I couldn't pull it off her, so I just pulled her.

'Don't! You're hurting!' she cried.

I wouldn't let go. 'Run! Run!' I yelled.

'Don't pull, then,' she whined.

I tried to be gentle but I could feel them getting closer. 'We've *got* to run,' I shouted, yanking at Polly's bag again.

With a scream Polly pitched forward and hit the pavement. Her bag split open and a pencil tin launched its contents across the road.

Polly's screaming turned to bitter sobs, and as I knelt to help her, the wolves swept up to us, one on either side. They looked down but their faces were in shadow. They were tall and muscular, their dark clothes skin-tight.

These wolves wore balaclava helmets and reflective glasses, and even in my panic I wondered what special sort of vision those lenses could provide in the dark.

I held tight to Polly and waited while they sailed round us. Round and round. There seemed to be no one else in the street.

'What d'you want?' I said, my voice catching in my throat.

They said nothing, just took a few more steps around us, tapping their rollerblades on the pavement. Cars passed by but no one stopped. Perhaps the drivers thought we were being helped, not hindered.

The tall, wordless circling began to stifle me. I felt that any minute they would close over us and we'd never breathe again. Tears began to blur my vision and that made me angry, so I opened my mouth and screamed.

'Laura!' A voice shouted.

The two figures melted away. They skimmed across the road like smoke, through a stream of hooting traffic. And then they were gone and Dad was kneeling beside us, lifting Polly while I gathered the bags and pencils.

We staggered a few yards and then we were home. Our gate had been so near but I had been too frightened to realize it.

Polly had grazed both her knees and the palm of her hand. She sat very still while Dad patched her up. 'They were so mean,' she kept saying. 'I hate them. I hate them.'

Gwendal had come down. He watched Dad dabbing and plastering Polly's wounds but he didn't say a word.

Dad murmured, 'I'm sorry Polly. So Sorry. I should have come to fetch you. Tomorrow I will.'

'Andy should have been with us,' I grumbled. 'He's selfish.'

But Dad told me that it wasn't Andy's fault. We couldn't expect him to give up his favourite sport.

'Laura made me run,' Polly complained. 'She pulled me. She's always pulling me these days. She knew it was going to happen. How did she know? And why have you got to stay with Gwendal all the time?'

Dad couldn't explain with Gwendal standing there, so quiet and anxious. 'I'll be there tomorrow,' he promised. 'And then we'll go and fetch Laura and Andy, or perhaps Mum can get the afternoon off and pick you up by car.'

'No,' Gwendal said suddenly. 'I'll come with you. Then we'll all be together and Mary won't have to know.'

Dad hadn't considered this. It seemed to worry him a little, but eventually he agreed. 'Look, Polly,' he said. 'Don't tell Mum about all this, will you?'

'Why?' asked Polly, who was dying to share her news with Mum.

'Because it would worry her, and we don't want that, do we?' Milo said sternly.

'But my bandages,' Polly protested.

'Tell her you fell over because I made you run,' I said. 'She'll understand.'

Dad threw me a grateful glance. 'I'm going to bring Lancelot indoors for the night,' he said. 'That's enough for Mum to worry about. They've promised a heavy frost.'

Next morning, as promised, the garden was white and crisp, and the wind seemed full of icicles.

Lancelot, hopping between our feet, took the edge off a rather tense breakfast. When Mum rushed off she was more concerned with Lancelot than Polly's wounds. 'He's eating the cables again,' she said. 'Please, please will someone put him out before he turns the freezer off.' (He did this once before and we lost a month's worth of shopping.)

As soon as Mum had gone Dad began to go through our afternoon routine. Andy must have been messing around with his rats because he wasn't in the kitchen. I was supposed to tell him but I had so much on my mind I forgot. Our paths didn't cross all day, unless you count a fleeting glimpse across the assembly hall.

When Dad turned up at the school gates with Gwendal and Polly in tow, Andy took one look at them and shouted, 'If you think I want to be seen walking home with my father and two little sisters, you're mad.' He didn't mention Gwendal or even look in his direction, he just took off speeding away from us without a backward glance. Milo didn't call after him. A group of boys were milling across the pavement in front of us and Dad didn't have the heart to humiliate Andy in their hearing.

The roads near our school are always busy in the afternoons, and it's only when we get close to our part of town that the crowds begin to thin out. Even so our street is seldom deserted, and on that afternoon there were several people walking on the other side.

We were halfway down the road, and passing the high wall of the health centre when we saw them. There was no mistaking the sinewy glide of the two tall figures.

'It's them,' I breathed.

'Go into the centre, quickly,' Milo commanded.

I clutched Gwendal and Polly's hands but I couldn't move.

'Laura!' Dad said urgently. 'I can deal with this.'

'There are two of them,' I whispered. 'You might need us.'

Dad started striding away from me towards the wolves. He appeared to be trying to identify them before he leapt into action. All at once, he grabbed hold of one and swung him round. The man hit out, but Dad was too quick, he ducked and punched.

There was a groan and the shadow staggered, but his companion swept round Milo, swung out his foot and kicked him in the back.

As Milo moaned and fell against the wall, I screamed, not as loudly as Polly, though. One of the wolves was gliding towards us. I tugged at the others and we ran into the drive behind us. I hated leaving Dad alone out there, but I knew I had to keep Gwendal safe. We pushed at the iron-barred gate and it slammed shut just as the wolf reached us. Polly was still screaming and a man appeared at the door of the health centre. 'What's up?' he called. The shadow rolled away from the gate, and fleetingly I thought, perhaps this was how ancient Milo met his end. His friends just couldn't reach him when the wolves closed in.

'It's my Dad,' I cried. 'He's being attacked.' I could hear this awful thumping, banging and grunting on the other side of the wall. 'Please help him.'

The stranger seemed a little reluctant to do this. He was overweight and clearly past his prime, but Polly's endless whimpering won him over. He swung back the gate and ran out. I rushed after him.

Milo, his head bent, was sitting with his back to the wall. A woman was already leaning over him when we got there. The wolves had vanished but Milo was very, very still.

'Dad! Dad!' I cried, terrified that he might never move again.

His raised his head and smiled at me.

'My God,' the fat man said. 'They've done quite a job on you.'

Milo's lip was cut, his cheekbone grazed and a clump of crazy hair was matted with blood.

'Thugs!' The woman declared. 'It's a disgrace. We can't even walk our own streets in peace.' I recognized her as our neighbour, Mrs Lennox. 'Tell the police, Mr McCool. I saw them. They don't scare me, the cowards. Did they get your wallet?'

Milo doesn't have a wallet but he pretended to feel for one. He shook his head, then, with a small grimace, carefully folded his arms across his ribs. 'They didn't get a thing, Mrs Lennox,' he said. 'I'll ring the police, though I didn't get a good look at them.'

'Cowards!' she repeated vehemently.

'Can you . . . move?' asked the fat man. 'I mean should we . . . an ambulance d'you think? The health centre's right there. I was waiting for my wife, as a matter of fact. It's her legs, they've swollen up again. Terrible to look at, can't wear her . . .'

Before the man could give us his wife's medical history, Dad said, 'No! No! I don't need an ambulance.' Then he turned and grappled with the wall, rather ineffectively.

'Goodness, Mr McCool, let me help.' Mrs Lennox slid her hand under Milo's shoulder and heaved, the fat man did the same. 'Just like *The Dark Knights* again, isn't it?' Mrs Lennox gave a strangled giggle of excitement.

Dad glanced at her, his mouth oddly twisted. 'It is indeed!' he said. 'Thank you! Thanks a lot. The kids'll help me home.' He grinned at me and then beyond me, and I turned to see that Gwendal and Polly had crept up to us. Polly was still shuddering with silent sobs. Gwendal had his arm round her shoulders, his face in the street-lit dusk was distant and desolate.

With much solicitous muttering, Mrs Lennox and the fat man straightened Dad up and brushed his jacket. Then they made their farewells and walked off together in the same direction, almost as if their meeting was pre-ordained.

We were alone with wolf-bitten Milo. When Polly grabbed his arm, he gave a small grimace of pain, then he tucked her hand in his.

Gwendal and I walked behind them. I glanced at Gwendal, but he was staring into a distance I couldn't even guess at. None of us said a word. Normally, Milo would have cracked a joke, but either his thoughts or his bruises were causing too much pain.

When we got home Andy was enjoying a small feast in the kitchen. Snow and Flake were on the table, sharing his slice of cake.

Andy's smile died when he saw Milo. Very slowly he got up, muttering, 'What happened?'

All my bottled up fear leapt out at him and I yelled, 'You were a lot of help!'

'What . . .' he murmured.

'They came again,' Polly whimpered. 'The roller-bladers. And Dad had a fight. You shouldn't have left us, Andy. We needed you.'

'Sorry.' Andy shuffled round the table. He picked up his rats and dropped them, one by one, into his pockets. 'I didn't know . . . did I? I'm sorry.'

Dad lowered himself into a chair. He seemed too exhausted even to think of speech. Gwendal sat close to him.

I put the kettle on and looked in the fridge for something to cook. Cheese seemed a good idea.

'Welsh rarebit,' I said blithely.

Andy said, 'I've had my tea,' and walked out, a hand in each pocket.

'Aren't you going to ring the police?' Polly asked.

'No.' Dad said.

'Why?' she demanded. 'You must. You must, must must. They'll help. It's twice now.'

'Polly, I can't identify them,' Milo murmured.

'I can,' said Polly. 'I remember exactly what they looked like. Every detail. Smokey colours they wore, and their faces were very white under those tight hat things.'

'Balaclavas,' I said.

'Yes,' she nodded. 'And Mrs Lennox saw them. So why don't you ring the police?'

'Because I've decided not to,' Milo said, with a touch of irritation.

'Well, I'm going to tell Mum,' Polly announced. '*She'll* know what to do.'

Milo gave resigned sigh.

I was the only one to see the angry bruises on his ribs, because I caught him coming from the bathroom with his clean shirt undone. He tried to cover them, but when he saw the look of horror on my face he grinned and said, 'Don't tell.'

But no one could keep the news from Mary this time. Milo's battered face told it all. Polly poured out the details with relish, exaggerating the horror, if that were possible, so that the sinister events were painted an even darker shade, and with a deeper ferocity.

'So much for the Dark Knight,' Mary said grimly.

'You should have seen the other fellow,' Milo told her, 'both of them. They didn't get off lightly.' But he had to endure her scolding while an examination of his cuts and bruises took place.

Everyone was keen to have an early night, but I crept downstairs for a glass of milk while Mum and Dad were still talking in the sitting-room. The television was on very low, and when I stood close to the door I could just make out their words.

Mum was angry. 'Look at you,' she said. 'Your hair is grey, you need specs to read with, and there's a metal pin in your leg.'

'Only one.' I imagined Milo's smile.

'Please, Milo,' Mum begged. 'Report those youths. They're ignorant thugs who've been paid to terrorize us. They don't know anything.'

Milo's voice was quieter and I found myself pressing my ear against the door. 'I can't take the risk,' he said. 'If the truth were known – he'd be lost.'

Mum was silent for a moment, then she said, 'Stop

this, Milo, please. Without you, we'll all be lost, Gwendal too.'

I couldn't hear his answer, but she gave a loud, exasperated sigh, and I crept up to bed without my milk.

Much later I found myself awake and not knowing why. I could hear traffic passing infrequently in the distance, but the house was silent. I remembered the glass of milk I'd promised myself and slipped downstairs. The living-room door was open and a cold draught on my feet made me look in. The french windows were slightly ajar.

The light from the street-lamps hardly reaches our garden, but that night the moon was full and very bright. The frost had already fallen and I realized that we'd forgotten to bring Lancelot indoors. Perhaps someone had come to fetch him.

And then I saw Gwendal. He was standing by the rabbit hutch, holding Lancelot close to his face, his cheek laid against the rabbit's head.

'Gwendal.' I tiptoed over the icy grass. 'You remembered Lancelot. You were the only one.'

He didn't say a word. His face in the dead light looked lifeless and remote.

'Let's take him in,' I said, stroking the rabbit's silky nose.

Gwendal followed me into the house and we pulled out Lancelot's spare box of hay and tucked him in with a carrot.

'He won't stay there, of course.' I smiled.

Gwendal didn't return the smile. His mouth was just a grim little line. He said nothing, and I shivered in the great void that lay around him, for it seemed to have swallowed even his words. I wanted to warm his small, cold hands and revive the pulse in him that seemed to be dying, but I found that I couldn't touch him. He knew this, I think, and walked away from me.

I stood in the warm kitchen until I heard a door close above me, and then I poured my glass of milk and took it up to bed. I felt ashamed.

Mum didn't go to work next day so we had the luxury of being ferried to school and back. The skaters were nowhere to be seen.

'Licking their wounds, no doubt,' Milo said gleefully.

Mum threw him a look that could have said, how many more wolves is it going to take?

On Saturday, Milo had to gake Gwendal to that very secret and private clinic for a check-up. When Gwendal came down to breakfast he wore the pressed white jeans and black anorak that he'd arrived in. We hadn't seen them since that first day.

'Are you still ill?' Polly asked him. 'Is that why you have to go back?'

He shook his head.

'It's just to make sure everything's all right,' Mum explained.

'Like what?' Polly pressed.

'Like how much he's grown, if we're feeding him the right stuff,' she smiled at Gwendal and I thought, it makes him sound like a rabbit.

Mum's answer seemed to satisfy Polly, however. 'The ratlets have grown,' she said. 'They're ginormous.'

'They'll have to go,' I heard Mum say, under her breath. Andy wasn't in the room.

Apart from the plaster on his cheek, Milo looked quite presentable; clean certainly. Mum had cut his hair and he'd shaved very carefully. Even the car had been cleaned. I followed Dad and Gwendal to the gate and waved goodbye.

Gwendal looked out from the passenger seat and lifted his hand. I couldn't be sure but I think he was smiling. When they'd gone I realized he hadn't said one word since the night of Dad's fight. I mentioned this to Mum but she didn't believe me.

'You'll probably remember something,' she said.

'You were at home all day, yesterday,' I reminded her. 'Did he talk to you?'

'No,' she admitted. 'He was very quiet, now I come to think of it.'

Milo didn't get home until late in the afternoon. It had been decided to keep Gwendal in the clinic overnight. 'I'll have to fetch him tomorrow,' Dad said.

'Is he ill, then?' I asked.

'No. Just more tests.'

'Did he talk to you, Dad?'

'No. He didn't seem able to.'

In the evening an icy rain turned briefly to snow and I began to think of Christmas. What could I get Gwendal that would make him smile?

I woke up with a sore throat but when I'd eaten a bowl of cereal I decided it wasn't that at all. It was just an ache that came from wanting to talk and not knowing what to say.

Dad came downstairs all spruced up for a second visit to the clinic, and then the telephone rang.

Mum picked up the receiver before an unwanted message could be dumped on the answerphone. She spent a long time saying nothing, and Dad called from the kitchen, 'Who is it?' He still lived in the hope of getting the odd part in a television drama, or a soap.

Mum said, 'I see. Yes, I understand. But where . . .? There's nothing we can do then, for now . . . Goodbye.' Something in her tone put me on my guard.

When Mum came into the kitchen she looked white and bewildered.

'So?' asked Milo. 'Anything important?'

'It was the clinic,' Mum said. 'Gwendal's gone.'

'Gone?' Milo didn't seem to comprehend.

Carefully, I lowered my spoon. We were alone in the kitchen, Mum, Dad and me.

'What d'you mean?' Dad's eyes were wide and afraid.

'He had another crisis. That's how they described it. So they contacted the sponsor and a car was sent, early this morning.'

'And they didn't think to contact us?' Dad exploded.

'It was forbidden, Milo. It was Gwendal's decision. He's gone to . . . to the person he belongs to.'

'He belongs to us,' cried Milo.

Mum took his arm. 'I know you're disappointed, but can't you see that it wasn't working? Culfire and his thugs . . .'

'Disappointed?' Milo repeated the word as though it were unknown to him.

'Don't look at me like that,' Mum begged. 'It had to end this way.'

'I'm going to find him,' he said.

Andy and Polly appeared in the doorway, alerted by the solemn conversation. They waited for us to enlighten them.

'Gwendal isn't coming home,' Dad told them, 'at least, not yet.'

Andy and Polly frowned, speechlessly.

If I hadn't read *The Little Prince* I might have felt as Mum did, that Gwendal was a lost cause. As it was I found myself thinking of the boy who fell to earth from a planet called B-612.

'He remembered Lancelot,' I said. 'He was the only one.'

Part Two

The fort

PART TWO

The Fact

1

Fort Saint-Luc

'Would you like another drink? Orange juice?'

Gwendal blinked up at the air hostess. His thoughts had been far away. Not even in the air. He shook his head. 'No thanks.'

She pushed her trolley away and Gwendal thought again of the message. *His* message. 'You are welcome. Of course you are. It is what I have always wanted. By the way, we have met, you and I.'

So why hadn't Gwendal recognized him? Surely he would have known the man whose skin and bones, whose genes had made him. He thought of all the people he had met: the doctors, scientists, psychologists, geneticists, technicians, paediatricians. Only a few had known who he was – what he was, and none of them had seemed related to him in any way.

He glanced at the woman beside him. Her eyes were closed and her heavy chin had dropped to her chest. He tapped her arm.

'Who will be meeting us?'

Mrs Carr opened her eyes. She'd been trying to catch up on her sleep. 'I've told you before. A man called Raoul.' She made an effort to hide her irritation but

Gwendal could tell that she'd been put out by this extra chore, the task of delivering him. There'd been no one else; no one who could be trusted, and even she didn't know the whole truth.

'Why won't it be him, my sponsor?'

'Gwendal, you've been told. He doesn't like to be recognized.'

'He could wear a wig, and a false moustache.'

'I expect he does, sometimes.' She managed to smile.

'How d'you know this Raoul will be the right person?'

Mrs Carr sighed. 'We have his photo, Gwendal.' She nodded at the print on Gwendal's knee. It showed a man with black eyes and heavy eyebrows. He was completely bald, and his smile revealed large crooked teeth. He looked neither honest, nor trustworthy.

'He could be an imposter,' Gwendal murmured.

'We have the password, Gwendal, the secret signal.' She winked, ineptly, and squeezed his hand.

He had thought of the words himself. Mrs Carr was to say, 'A good day to meet, Monsieur,' and Raoul must answer, 'Not for wolves, Madame!' Of course, neither of them had the slightest idea why Gwendal had chosen these strange lines. He'd been thinking of Milo when they slipped into his head; Milo and Laura. It was Laura who had told him about the wolves, who kept on and on about them, in fact. How they were biting into Milo, chewing him up, until soon there'd be no Milo at all. And it was true. Gwendal couldn't get Milo's damaged face out of his mind: the bruises and the blood. And it was all on his account. It was his fault.

He'd made his mind up long before they reached the

clinic. It had been hard saying goodbye, knowing that, in a way, he was betraying Milo. But also saving him. Gwendal smiled to himself.

'That's better.' Mrs Carr had noticed his smile. 'I was beginning to wonder if you really wanted to make this journey.'

'Oh yes,' said Gwendal. 'But I shall miss them. My . . . family.'

'There'll be other children where you're going, I believe. You'll soon make friends again.'

'Yes.' But the thought of starting all over again made Gwendal feel tired. It had taken so long to become a McCool, to believe he was part of the family. Only Laura had tried to understand, apart from Milo and Mary. Kind, funny Laura, rushing into problems, saying things she shouldn't, thoughtful and fierce. He had betrayed her too. He should have told her what he had decided to do. He should have said goodbye.

'Look, Gwendal. We're nearly there!' Mrs Carr nodded at the window and Gwendal looked out to see green swathes of land appear through the drifting clouds. Now clusters of houses could be seen beside thin grey roads and bare trees.

The plane swung down and in a few moments they were bumping over the runway.

No going back now. Soon I shall know who I am. Gwendal's stomach clenched uncomfortably. Do I want to know?

The man appeared while they were waiting to reclaim the bags. You couldn't miss him; his eyebrows were so thick, his head so round and naked. He wasn't tall but gave the impression of immense strength. A good man to have on your side. He didn't return Gwendal's tentative smile. He merely lifted his hand and nodded.

Gwendal, chilled by the man's expression, turned his attention to the luggage. Mrs Carr had already seen his bag. She swung it to the ground, saying, 'You haven't brought much, Gwendal.'

'Mrs Carr, he's here!' Gwendal glanced over at the man who was now walking towards them.

'Ah! Monsieur . . .? Raoul?'

'Madame Carr!'

They shook hands and the secret exchange took place.

'It's a good day to meet, Monsieur!'

'Not for wolves, Madame!'

Gwendal had to giggle because Raoul's accent was so odd. It made the words into something quite different. 'Natfair wollffs!'

Neither of the adults found it funny.

Mrs Carr walked out into the winter sunshine with them. She spoke in French but Gwendal understood most of it. She told Raoul that the boy was well, but tired. He must have a rest when he got to *the place*. He would probably be hungry. He was excited but nervous.

Raoul nodded silently and glanced at Gwendal from time to time.

They reached a dark red vehicle, possibly a Land Rover, Gwendal wasn't sure. And Mrs Carr suddenly did something very surprising. She bent down and pecked at Gwendal's cheek.

'Goodbye, Gwendal,' she said. 'Good luck!' Then she walked away without a backward glance.

Gwendal, who had always been alone, felt more alone than ever before. Raoul didn't like him. It was obvious.

He hadn't noticed the boys, peering from the back seat. When he stepped up into the car, he saw two grinning faces.

' 'Ullo!' said the nearest boy, moving up to give Gwendal space.

'Hullo!' Gwendal stared at the boys. They were very alike; dark-eyed with thick brown hair.

The boy next to Gwendal was an inch or two taller than the other. 'I am Alain,' he said. 'We speak English with you!'

Gwendal nodded and shook the boy's extended hand.

'My name is Jacques,' said the smaller boy, parrot-like, and with a huge smile.

'*Mon frère*,' added Alain.

'My name is Gwendal,' Gwendal replied.

When Raoul started the car and they began the long journey to 'the fort,' as Alain called it, Gwendal had made two friends. His relief was immense. He wouldn't have to spend hours alone with surly Raoul, trying to think of something to say.

Alain and Jacques spoke halting English but they had brought a dictionary with them, and soon the three boys were chattering and laughing together. No one would have guessed they had only just met. They described their village and the fort in so much detail, that by the time they reached the foothills of the Pyrenees, Gwendal felt he knew exactly what to expect. But nothing could prepare him for the real thing.

As they climbed higher, sudden views of gleaming

peaks would drag Gwendal's attention away from his friends, and he would exclaim, 'It's amazing! It's fantastic – beautiful.'

Alain and Jacques grinned happily. 'Yes,' they agreed. 'It's beautiful.' But it was their home and therefore not as amazing to them as Gwendal found it.

At last they reached a small town tucked in the shadow of a massive cliff. The rocks that rose behind the town were hung with scrubby grass and patches of snow. Soon it would be all ice, the boys said.

They came to a square surrounded by squat trees, their twisted branches hung with fairy lights. The car stopped and Alain said, 'This is Saint-Luc. We say good-bye now.' He shook Gwendal's hand once more, and then both boys jumped out and ran off between the bare trees, turning to wave before they disappeared into a grey three-storey building.

As soon as they had gone, Raoul drove out of the square and Gwendal found himself looking down on a wide icy river. They crossed a bridge and then the big vehicle began to roar up a narrow track to the top of the cliff. The track widened and became a snowfield, and Gwendal, squinting into the dusk, saw his new home: Fort Saint-Luc.

Alain and Jacques had tried to tell him, but their description had failed to convey the atmosphere here; ancient bricks built into rock, tiny windows winking like stars, and a door that could have been a thousand years old. Fort Saint-Luc was part of a mountain.

Raoul parked beside the door and said, 'You here now.'

A lantern hanging in the vaulted porch swung gently as Gwendal opened the car door and climbed out. It was icy cold and he began to shiver. The shiver travelled deep into his bones and he had to clench his jaw against his rattling teeth. He stood in the damp porch while Raoul drove the car round to a garage beside the fort, and he wished he was at home with Milo and Mary.

And then the big door swung inwards and Gwendal found himself looking at someone he knew.

'Dr Zeigler,' he breathed. His relief was so enormous he flung himself into the old man's arms. 'I didn't know you'd be here.'

'I'm sorry, Gwendal.' Dr Zeigler hugged him back. 'I couldn't tell you. It had to be a secret.'

So many secrets, but now it didn't matter.

'You know my . . . *him*, then?' he said.

'Yes, I know him.'

Dr Zeigler led Gwendal into a vast circular room. Even from the doorway he could feel the heat from logs burning in the huge fireplace. The room glowed with soft light from table-lamps and candles, and Gwendal saw that the walls were unpainted rock and stone. As his gaze travelled upwards he found himself staring at night clouds, rolling above him through a deep blue sky. The domed roof was made of glass.

'It's amazing,' he murmured.

'My retreat,' said Dr Zeigler. 'My eyrie.'

'Yours?' said Gwendal, 'I thought . . .'

'Mine,' said Dr Zeigler, 'and yours, Gwendal.'

Something dawned in Gwendal's mind, and then Raoul came in, speaking French in short impatient sentences. He crossed the room and disappeared behind a velvet curtain.

'In a moment Raoul will bring you something to eat,' said Dr Zeigler, 'but now we will make ourselves comfortable together, and talk.'

They sat on a squeaky leather chesterfield before the fire, and while Gwendal stared into the flames, Dr Zeigler revealed his true identity.

At first Gwendal felt cheated. He wished he had known right from their first meeting who Dr Zeigler really was. But he realized that he couldn't remember that meeting. The doctor had always been in his life. Every few weeks he would arrive at the clinic with a new game, or a book, and they would walk together in the garden and talk. And later there had been weekend trips into the country and to the sea, anywhere he wanted to go – except to a city.

'So you're my sponsor?' Gwendal said at last. 'I'm glad.'

'Sponsor sounds a little commercial, doesn't it? Shall we use the word "guardian"?'

'If you like.'

'I have another name, too. My real name.'

'Why did you change it?' asked Gwendal.

'Too many people know me by my real name. I suppose I am what you would call famous, Gwendal.' The doctor gave a sort of sigh as if he were not completely happy about being who he was.

'So who are you?' Gwendal demanded.

'My name is Jean Tisseyre.'

Gwendal was disappointed. He had never heard the name, and said so.

Jean laughed, and his whole face emerged from its formal mask. 'No, I'm not a pop star, or even a movie director,' he said. 'But the banks have heard of me, the multinationals, the world of commerce. I'm not very popular in some quarters, I'm afraid. I make too much money. I seem to have a gift for it.' He laughed again.

'Oh.' Gwendal was tempted to ask if the same thing would happen to him, considering they were, in a way, the same person. But he couldn't bring himself to speak of their peculiar relationship. For some reason he found it embarrassing; distasteful even.

Raoul appeared with a supper tray which he slid, rather ungraciously, on to a low table in front of Gwendal.

'Soup!' he said curtly, and turned away before Gwendal could thank him.

'Do you have a wife . . . or someone?' Gwendal asked Jean, hoping a motherly sort of person might be tucked away somewhere, in a room that was like Mary's, warm and pretty.

'I'm afraid not,' said Jean. 'She died a long, long time ago, when I was still a young man. Her name was Véronique.'

'I like that,' said Gwendal. He remembered the woman in the virtual reality programme. She, too, was Véronique. But wasn't she Jean's mother?

'One day I'll tell you about her.'

'Raoul doesn't like me,' Gwendal whispered as he saw the velvet curtain twitch slightly.

'That's not true,' Jean told him. 'Your sudden appearance was a shock to him. He's not usually so thoughtless. He is a little wary of strangers.'

'Didn't he know about me?'

'Yes, he knew. But let us say, he did not exactly approve of what I . . . of the way you were brought into the world.'

Gwendal knew this was an opportunity to probe; to ask an enormous question; the reason for his existence, and why Jean had wanted to reproduce himself. But he shrank from the question. He was not ready to know the answer.

Instead it was Jean who inquired, 'Why are you here, Gwendal?'

The real reason could not be given. Gwendal had to make Jean believe he wanted to be here, with him, more than anything in the world. So he wouldn't tell him about Nathan Culfire, the angel hunter, and the terrible danger he had brought to the McCools, especially Milo, Milo more than anyone.

He said, 'I thought it was time. I wanted to be with the person who is my . . . I wanted to be with you.'

He began to drink the soup and found it surpris-ingly delicious. Jean sat watching him and Gwendal remembered how Dr Zeigler had often watched him in this way. Was he trying to recall every moment of what it was like to be a boy again, even down to the tasting of soup?

After supper Jean took Gwendal into the room that had been prepared for him. It couldn't have been furnished overnight. Jean must have been hoping for such an occasion for a long time. Gwendal was overwhelmed by the size of the room. One side was filled with equipment. As well as a computer and all the gadgets a boy could want, the wall was entirely covered by closed circuit TV monitors. Gwendal could see the great circular hall, the kitchen (where Raoul was chopping something bloody), several rooms and passages, the front door, and the track leading up to the fort.

'You see you are safe,' Jean said. 'No thief or intruder can reach you without being seen.'

'Do you expect them to try?' asked Gwendal.

Jean laughed. 'No, Gwendal. It's just in case.'

'I'll get lost in that bed,' Gwendal remarked, eyeing the huge four-poster on the other side of the room. And then, before Jean could reply, he saw Isidore. He was standing on the bedside table, his round head shining in the light of a large table-lamp.

'Isidore!' cried Gwendal, rushing to the little figure. 'They've changed your eyes.' For the robot's eyes were now a pale blue.

'This is Isambard,' said Jean. 'A good name for Isidore's twin, don't you agree? I'll show you what he can do.'

Gwendal handed over the little robot and Jean demonstrated Isambard's many abilities. Most important of all, to Gwendal, was Isambard's link with Isidore. They could send messages to each other and display them on their tiny screens or on one of the monitors on Gwendal's wall.

'I could talk to Laura,' Gwendal said, perching on the big bed, 'and tell her where I am.'

'Talk, by all means, Gwendal. But don't let her know where you are.'

'I can trust her,' Gwendal insisted.

'I'm sure you can. But for now your whereabouts must remain secret. You must tell no one.'

Jean Tisseyre was used to being obeyed, and his tone reminded Gwendal that he was far away from the people he loved. He frowned at Isambard, trying not to show his anxiety.

But Jean had noticed and, ruffling Gwendal's hair, he said gently, 'You are tired. Tomorrow you will speak with your friend, Laura. Raoul has brought your case, you see? So you can sleep now.'

'She's my sister,' Gwendal said.

Jean looked puzzled.

'Laura. She's my sister.'

'Of course. Your sister.' Jean smiled. 'Do you need anything else? A drink perhaps?'

Gwendal shook his head.

'Good night, then, *mon petit*!' Jean put his arms round Gwendal and kissed his head. 'If you need me, just come and call.'

Milo's good-night hug had folded round Gwendal, warm and tight, like a bear. Jean had arms that didn't fold, they bent uncomfortably, and Gwendal thought, he hasn't had much practice in hugging.

As he watched the tall figure walk to the door, Gwendal felt a distance yawn between them, and a voice told him that he would never be that lonely old man.

He found it difficult to sleep. At first he watched the flickering screens, and when his eyes began to ache he turned his back on them. But their light still swam round the room, so he jumped out of bed and turned them off, one by one, until he reached the last. The screen was blank, but Gwendal stared at it, hopefully. Perhaps Isidore would send a message.

A shadowy image appeared on the surface; a pale figure with a mysterious face. His own reflection.

Gwendal crept back to bed. He hadn't been troubled by nightmares since he had lived with his family, even when Culfire had been about. Before that, they had been very bad. The worst one was not even a dream. It was a memory, and Gwendal could feel it now, edging its way into his head.

On his ninth birthday Milo and Mary didn't visit Gwendal. He was told that one of their other children was in a school play that couldn't be missed. He had felt left out, worse, the thought crept into his mind that he was a mistake. He had grown up believing that Milo and Mary were his true parents. And then, slowly, it had dawned on him that he was different. He could never go home because he was at risk, they said. But it wasn't just that. Something was horribly wrong.

That night he stole the keys to one of the laboratories. It was in a separate block, across the courtyard from the main building. Gwendal chose the most secure and inaccessible of all the laboratories. He knew that a hundred rats and mice lived there. Animals that were weighed and measured and watched, like him. Animals that were sometimes dissected.

He had opened every cage, and if the animals did not tumble out, he lifted them gently to the floor. They swarmed over his feet and ran along his arms, they nestled against his neck and nibbled his fingers: sad creatures that didn't know what they were; experiments. Like him. That's when he had begun to guess.

One of the technicians saw a light and burst into the

room. The sight of Gwendal, standing there, alive with animals, must have terrified the man. Seizing a broom he had rushed at Gwendal, brushing the creatures away from him. One of them, a huge white rat, suddenly leapt at the broom-head and sank its teeth into the handle.

The man swung the broom against a cabinet, but the rat clung on.

'Don't!' cried Gwendal, trying to pull the broom away.

He was pushed aside and fell against a steel cabinet. From the floor he watched, helplessly, as the technician dashed the rat against a metal table-leg until the creature dropped lifeless to the floor.

'You've killed it,' cried Gwendal, 'and it didn't do anything. It didn't hurt me.'

'It was diseased, you stupid boy,' growled the man.

The noise had alerted other staff and soon the laboratory was crowded with angry scientists. Dr Mac was called, a gentle soft-spoken man with a mop of strawlike hair. Gwendal knew him better than anyone else at the clinic. He had brought Gwendal into the world, so Milo said.

Gwendal was hysterical when the doctor appeared. Gently, Mac led the boy away from the mayhem he had caused.

'It wasn't your fault,' Mac told Gwendal. 'you mustn't think that. Old Ratty would have died very soon. He was ill.'

'Who made him ill?' sobbed Gwendal.

'I don't know anything about it, Gwendal. It's not my department.'

'This is a horrible place!' Gwendal said.

Next day Mac had called him out of a lesson. There happened to be several children of his age at the clinic that week, and Gwendal had enjoyed their company.

'Good luck,' whispered one of the boys. 'Are you going to have an op?'

'Don't think so,' Gwendal whispered back.

Mac took him to his room and told him that his sponsor had been contacted.

'I think you've had a crisis, Gwendal,' Mac said. 'And we agree, your sponsor and I, that it's time for you to leave here.'

'Leave?' Gwendal was at once amazed and a little scared. 'Where will I go?'

'We think you should decide. Milo and Mary have children and you might prefer their company to that of . . . well, someone who is getting on in years. On the other hand, your sponsor has a beautiful home. He's rich and you would have everything you could want. And you would be safer.'

'Safe from what?' Gwendal asked.

Mac shrugged. 'You are a special boy, Gwendal. A little different from others. There may be risks attached to your being . . . in the world at large.'

'I'd be safe with Milo.'

2

Christmas

Gwendal woke early, before dawn, and was standing by his window when the sun came up. The white, fairytale mountains were bathed in colour. It was beautiful, special. He wished Laura were there to see it with him.

He waited until Raoul came to fetch him for breakfast, not daring to explore the place on his own. Afterwards Jean took him for a walk. They wore snow boots, thick anoraks and woollen hats. Gwendal's were black, his favourite colour. Jean wore scarlet.

Jean told Gwendal about the Cathars who had once lived in the fort. He showed him where they had been burned to death, every one of them, apart from those who had thrown themselves off the mountain. They were killed for defying the Pope, and for believing in a Prince of Darkness. Gwendal found some of the reasoning hard to follow. He thought again of asking the question. But he couldn't.

After lunch Jean disappeared into his study, and Gwendal was left to entertain himself. He went to his room to put Isambard to use. The thought that he hadn't said goodbye to Laura weighed heavily.

It took only a few seconds for Isambard to make

contact. Displayed on the monitor was Isidore's view of Gwendal's room in London. He pressed the keys that Jean had demonstrated. Now he could hear Isidore's signal. Click! Click! Click! But no one could hear him. Refusing to give up, Gwendal continued pressing the same three keys. He was about to abandon the computer when Laura's face swam into view.

She frowned at Isidore's lens, turned her head a little and said, 'It's me. Laura.'

It was good to hear her voice, even though she sounded rather fierce. That was just Laura.

Gwendal pressed Isambard's message signal.

'Where?' asked Laura.

Look on the monitor, idiot! Gwendal smiled to himself. He wrote, 'LAURA. I DIDN'T SAY GOODBYE. I'M SORRY.'

'Gwendal! Where are you?' Her big grey eyes grew wider.

He couldn't tell her and didn't know how to answer. It occurred to him that he could speak directly to her, but he didn't trust his voice. This way was better.

'GWENDAL! ARE YOU THERE?' she demanded.

'YES.'

'WHY DID YOU LEAVE US?'

She must know why, he thought. 'I COULDN'T STAY,' he wrote.

'WHY NOT?'

Surely she remembered those bruises on her father's face? The blood. 'IT WAS TOO DANGEROUS.'

'NO. WE WOULD HAVE WORKED IT OUT. MILO COULD HAVE FIXED THEM ALL.'

For a moment Gwendal was taken aback by the force of her words. Did she really miss him, then? Could it be that she liked him enough to face the danger? He wrote, 'NOT WITHOUT . . .' then, thinking of the savage beating Milo suffered, he added 'PAIN.'

Laura didn't answer this. Instead she put the question, 'ARE YOU HAPPY, WHERE YOU ARE?'

How could he truthfully answer that? He wrote, 'I THINK I SHALL BE. GOODBYE LAURA.' And then something made him add, 'GIVE ISIDORE TO ANDY.' Because Andy might be able to decipher the message that Isidore still held.

'ANDY? WHY HIM?' asked Laura.

Gwendal couldn't explain. He wanted them to find him, he realized. He couldn't lose his family entirely, and instinct told him that Andy was the one most likely to sit for hours exploring Isidore's memory.

He watched Laura's questions appear on the screen. Questions he couldn't answer. At length he turned away and left the room, taking Isambard with him.

Jean met him in the round hall. 'You've made friends, then?' he said, nodding at the robot clutched in Gwendal's hand.

'Oh, yes,' Gwendal said. But he didn't tell Jean what they had been up to, he and Isambard. And Jean didn't ask.

They sat together before a glowing fire, and Gwendal gazed up at the domed roof. It was already dark and a constellation of bright stars filled the circle of glass.

Jean wanted to know more about the family Gwendal had decided to leave, especially Milo. And Gwendal found himself saying, 'He needs some acting work, you know. He's a fantastic house-father, but it would be good if he could work sometimes, and earn some money.'

'I see.' Jean stared thoughtfully at the leaping flames. 'I didn't realize.'

'I thought you knew all about them,' Gwendal said accusingly.

'Not everything,' Jean admitted. 'It was your progress I followed, not theirs.'

'Well, do you think you could do something about Milo? He's still in good shape, and he's got a great voice. If you've got all this wealth and influence and everything, couldn't you make things happen?'

'Yes,' Jean said. 'I could.'

Raoul appeared with a tray of food. This time he wasn't so grim-faced; he even managed to smile in Gwendal's direction.

After supper they played the French version of Monopoly. 'To help with your French,' Jean said. 'You will find it easier in school, if your French is good.'

Gwendal hadn't thought of that. Would he be going to school, then? He had always wanted to be like other children. But a French school. 'Will Alain and Jacques be in this school I'm going to?'

'Of course.'

So that would be all right then.

'It's probably time for you to go to bed,' Jean said. 'I'm afraid I remember very little about the habits of children.'

'Me too.' Gwendal grinned.

Perhaps now it was time for the question. But the moment passed and the question was not put.

'Can I go outside, just for a few minutes?' he asked Jean.

'I will come with you,' Jean said.

But he only came as far as the step. He stood watching Gwendal, as the boy walked out onto the snowfield. When he was a few metres away from the fort, Gwendal held Isembard before him. Would anyone be there, he wondered? At home in London? Would they see this place; the mountains standing like carved ice under the moon, the black chasm that lay before him and the dark pines dotting the slopes beyond? 'Laura, see this,' Gwendal implored. 'See where I am.'

He turned back to the tall figure under the lantern.

It was surprising how fast the days flew after that. Two days later, Alain and Jacques arrived with their father, Gérard Bezain. Gwendal felt immediately at ease. Gérard reminded him of Milo; the warm easy laugh, the impression of strength he conveyed, of protectiveness.

The Bezains took Gwendal to their home, a tall house full of noisy dogs and children. There were three girls as well as Alain and Jacques, and a mother with long brown hair and eyes the colour of almonds. They kept their promise to teach Gwendal to ski, and a few days later a new ski suit arrived, and small silver skis. Jean came to watch Gwendal's first hesitant movements, but after that he left him in Gérard's care.

'I'd trust Gérard with my life,' Jean said.

Gwendal thought, I suppose my life is yours. And again the question popped into his mind, and once again was left unasked.

Days of action and excitement were followed by quiet evenings alone with Jean. Sometimes Jean was busy, and then Raoul would join Gwendal. They played board games together, and Gwendal eventually became used to Raoul's heavy grunts as he shook the dice or moved his counter, the howls of protest when he lost a game.

Raoul seemed to have overcome his aversion to Gwendal. He smiled a great deal now, showing a row of crooked but exceedingly white teeth. The fears that had caused his cold hostility had obviously been dispelled.

In schoolboy French, Gwendal tried to describe the McCools. He wanted Raoul to know them, especially Laura whom Gwendal felt he knew best. He wanted Raoul to recognize her in case . . . in case. Would she ever come to Fort Saint-Luc?

Sometimes Gwendal took Isambard out into the snow, or left him to record the objects in his room. He wanted the McCools to have a picture of his life.

A few days before Christmas Madame Bezain took Gwendal shopping. They wandered round the small shops that bordered the square, and Gwendal bought a woollen scarf for Jean and thick walking socks for Raoul. He was happy until he saw the angel.

He wanted to send his other family a card and was about to choose a bright tree, sprinkled with glitter, when the angel slipped forward and fell at his feet. It was a beauti-ful angel: a little boy, blowing a trumpet, each feather on his small white wings outlined in gold. Gwendal stared at it in horror, and then he turned and stumbled out of the shop.

Madame Bezain ran after him, calling, 'Gwendal! *Qu'est que c'est?*'

Tears were falling from his eyes; a great flood of them.

The glowing white bulbs strung across the trees were distorted into blocks of light. They lifted and swung like blazing angelic wings, and Gwendal's sobs tore through his chest.

'What is it, *chérie*? What happened?' Madame Bezain's arms closed round him. 'Ssh! Ssh! What is it?'

Gwendal shook his head, again and again, trying to rid himself of tears. 'The angel,' he gasped. 'I'm not . . . I'm not . . .' But nothing more would come.

He was taken home and Madame Bezain described what had happened to a concerned Jean Tisseyre.

Gwendal couldn't explain himself. But when Madame Bezain had gone, he did manage to put a question, rather crossly, to Jean. One of his contact lenses had washed away with the falling tears, and he had to use the spectacles he so hated.

'When I was . . . was conceived . . . why didn't you give me better eyesight?' he asked. 'I thought they could do that. And why aren't I stronger, and not clumsy. I am clumsy, you know . . . and although I'm good at maths, I'm no good at drawing things, or music. I've tried but it just won't come. Even Polly can play a flute. And I'm a coward, I know I am.'

Jean frowned at Gwendal. He looked troubled and unsure. 'I wanted you, Gwendal, only you, just as you are and not changed in any way. Aren't you happy as you are?'

Gwendal honestly didn't know.

'Why did the picture of an angel upset you? Can't you tell me?'

Jean's face looked desperately weary. His dark eyes

were almost hidden in their gaunt, shadowy sockets. Gwendal couldn't bring himself to tell such a tired old man that the angel had reminded him of the reason he had come to France. That he had fled from his family to save Milo from the angel hunter. That, perhaps, he was homesick. And there was more that he couldn't explain, even to himself.

With sudden insight, Jean said, 'He's working, you know. Your Milo. It's what you wanted, isn't it?'

'Thank you!' Gwendal breathed, and at last he flung himself into Jean's arms.

On Christmas Eve they attended a midnight mass in the little church in Saint-Luc. Jean, Raoul and Gwendal were squeezed tight between four generations of the Bezain family. There were two sets of grandparents, a great-grandmother and numerous sets of aunts, uncles and cousins. The church glittered with candles and behind the altar, a stained glass angel stood before the Virgin Mary. Its wings were huge and beautiful, but this time Gwendal didn't cry.

He woke very late on Christmas day, and found a basket of presents by his bed, all from Jean and Raoul: there were chocolates and toys, computer games and clothes. Nothing from his family.

They don't know where I am, he told himself. When he tried to imagine Christmas in River Street he could almost hear their voices, singing and laughter. He wished he'd had the courage to go back into that shop; to walk past the angel and reach for the card with the bright tree.

After breakfast Jean suggested a walk. This time Raoul came with them. They climbed the steep snowfields behind the fort. The snow blazed in the sunlight and they all wore dark glasses. Raoul began to sing in a rich bass voice, and with a sudden burst of happy energy Gwendal bounded away, over a ridge of snow-covered rocks.

'Hi!' called Raoul. 'Gwendal!'

Gwendal glanced back. Raoul was still climbing, but Jean stood looking up at him, and it struck Gwendal how helpless he looked; how sad. Gwendal sat in the snow and with a cheerful yell, slid and stumbled back to them.

That evening Gwendal helped Raoul prepare for their Christmas feast. The long oak table looked splendid; silver dishes and crystal goblets sparkled in the candlelight. The plates were edged with gold and beside each place Raoul put a tiny package, tied with red silk ribbons. '*Père Noel,*' he told Gwendal with a wink.

While Raoul was in the kitchen, making the final preparations, Jean and Gwendal sat before the fire and shared a glass of wine. Gwendal was glad to see that Jean's pale face had taken on a healthy glow, but all at once, the old man looked very solemn and, leaning close to Gwendal, he asked, 'What do you want most in the world, Gwendal?'

Taken by surprise, Gwendal said, 'More than anything?'

'More than anything.'

Gwendal thought of his family: he badly wanted to see them. He thought of Culfire and wished the angel hunter were dead. But most of all he wanted the answer to one question.

'I want to know the reason for my existence,' he said gravely.

'The reason?' Jean smiled thoughtfully. 'Of course.'

'Why did you want more of yourself?'

'Myself?' Jean looked puzzled.

'Me,' said Gwendal. 'I'm just you all over again. Why? Why would anyone want more of themselves?'

'But I didn't,' Jean said. And then he told Gwendal the truth.

Gwendal had been prepared for a description of compli-cated procedures that he might not fully compre-hend. But the explanation, when it came, was not like that. It was easy to understand, but infinitely more terrible.

Perhaps Jean didn't realize how much his story had shocked Gwendal. When he left the room to see how the meal was progressing, Gwendal took Isambard out of his pocket. He carried the robot across to the table and recorded the candlelit spread.

When that was done, he left the hall and filmed his walk out to the passage. He took his black jacket from a hook and, placing Isambard on a chair, he pulled on the jacket. Then he opened the great oak door and descended the steps on to the snow.

As he moved away from the shelter of the fort, the wind rushed at him and he staggered from its force. The air was charged with flying particles of ice, and ragged shadows tore across the ground as the moon battled with the clouds.

In a white daze, Gwendal threw one arm across his face, the other out before him. And Isambard flew from his grasp, his bright eyes still faithfully recording what he saw.

Gwendal stumbled onwards. He had thought he knew who he was, but he had been misled. He wished with all his heart that he had not uncovered the truth.

Part Three

The last wolf

1
Lost

You could be forgiven for thinking that was the end of it. That trying to find someone who didn't want to be found was pointless, especially if most people considered him best forgotten. But then you don't know Milo McCool like I do. I knew the story of Gwendal had only just begun.

Nathan Culfire, who had been the enemy, was now an impotent wolf, merely an irritation. He came at tea-time and Milo gave a smug grin when he saw him approaching the window.

'Where is he?' were Mr Culfire's first words when Milo opened the door. No greetings, no thanks for allowing him a second chance to criticize our home.

'He's gone,' we heard Milo say. 'Forgive me but I haven't finished my tea.' He turned away but Mr Culfire pursued him, slamming the front door behind him.

When Milo came into the kitchen, Culfire was leering over his shoulder. He was as difficult to shake off as a slug.

'Where?' said Culfire. 'Where have you hidden him?'

'Surely you know, Mr Culfire. You must have followed me yesterday. You knew I took him to a certain clinic and left him there. So you must know he isn't here.' Milo gave him a cold smile.

Nathan Culfire's small eyes contracted into mean black dots.

'You're welcome to search the house,' Milo said.

Mum glanced up anxiously but Mr Culfire declined. He stood looking down at us and the memory of the silent, circling wolves made me feel ill. I pushed my plate away and closed my eyes.

'And while we're about it,' went on Milo, 'tell your thugs to keep away from my children. If they come anywhere near them, I shall have them put behind bars – you too, come to that!'

'I thought you preferred to take the law into your own hands, Mr McCool,' said Culfire, eyeing the plaster on Dad's wounded cheek. 'You know what will happen if you report the incident.'

'We've nothing to hide.' Mum, who'd been pouring tea, suddenly stood up. 'The boy's gone. Go and look for him.'

'Where am I to look, Mrs McCool?' Culfire spread his hands. 'Give me a clue, won't you?'

'He's with the person he belongs to,' Mum said.

Mr Culfire looked shaken. 'Him? *Him*? I don't believe this!'

'It's true,' she said, 'and as we don't know who he is or where he lives, you probably have a better idea of his whereabouts than we do. Now, please leave my house, because quite frankly Mr Culfire, you give me the creeps!' She sat down, drained by the effort of talking to him.

'How did this come about?' Culfire wanted to know.

'You drove him to it, Mr Culfire,' Milo said. 'He decided that living with us was bad for his health, and ours. So he's gone somewhere safer, to someone who is powerful enough to protect him.'

Nathan Culfire gave Milo a withering look and left. But the smell of him remained; an aftermath of decay lingered in our kitchen and I couldn't stand being in the same room with it. How could a man who smelt so bad be the guardian of angels? I covered my nose and mouth with my hand, so that I shouldn't inhale one tiny breath of him.

'What is it, Laura?' Mum said.

'The smell,' I mumbled. 'Like rotten eggs.'

'Sulphur,' Milo commented.

'Why does he smell so bad?' asked Polly.

'Because he's old,' Andy told her.

Polly thought about this for a moment and then remarked, 'But he's got black hair.'

'The only part of him that's alive,' Mum said grimly. 'He's just a fanatical old cadaver. It's pathetic.'

'Fanatics are always dangerous,' Milo murmured, staring into his tea.

I left them and ran upstairs. As I was passing Gwendal's room I heard a familiar clicking. I opened the door and my eye fell on Isidore. Gwendal had left him behind. This seemed so unlikely. Could he have known he was going somewhere so safe he wouldn't need Isidore? Or were they lying, the people who said it had been Gwendal's decision? Perhaps he had been taken somewhere against his will.

I became aware that the little robot was trying to tell me something. 'Mmm! Ahhh! Mmm!'

'It's me,' I said. 'Laura.'

'Mmm.' Isidore repeated. His eyes flashed. 'MESSAGE' said the tiny screen below his head.

'Where?' I looked at the computer screen and a message began to appear. 'LAURA. I DIDN'T SAY GOODBYE. I'M SORRY.'

'Gwendal! Where are you?'

For seconds I waited. No reply.

I bent over the keyboard and spelled out my message. 'GWENDAL! ARE YOU THERE?'

'YES.' Nothing more.

'WHY DID YOU LEAVE US?'

'I COULDN'T STAY.'

'WHY NOT?'

'IT WAS TOO DANGEROUS.'

'NO WE WOULD HAVE WORKED IT OUT. MILO COULD HAVE FIXED THEM ALL.'

'NOT WITHOUT . . .' There was a pause before the word, 'PAIN,' appeared.

I didn't know how to reply to this, because in a way it was true, so I said, 'ARE YOU HAPPY, WHERE YOU ARE?'

Another long hesitation, before Gwendal answered, 'I THINK I SHALL BE. GOODBYE LAURA. GIVE ISIDORE TO ANDY.'

'Andy? Why him?' I spoke aloud as I pressed the keys.

Gwendal didn't answer. I tried other questions, words, phrases, anything to know that wherever he was, he was still in touch. But there was nothing.

'FINISH' said Isidore's screen.

'Is that information, or are you giving me an order?' I asked angrily.

Isidore blinked. 'GONE' he tried.

'OK. I'm sorry.' I printed out our brief conversation and took it down to the kitchen. 'This came,' I said. 'A message from Gwendal. We talked for a bit, and then he went.'

Dad took the paper, frowning over the words as he read them. Mum looking over his shoulder, said, 'It's hardly a message.'

'Not even a thank you,' I said, sort of as a joke.

'Why should be thank us?' Milo said. 'What did we give him that he didn't deserve?' He changed the subject. 'So, he's left Isidore to Andy.'

'Me?' Andy looked up. 'Really, me? He's left his robot to me?'

'I can't think why,' I said. And then I realized that it was probably one of the cleverest things Gwendal could have done. The gift of Isidore would win over the one member of our family who was not entirely on his side. It must mean that he intended to come back.

Andy ran upstairs. A moment later he came back with Isidore. 'It's a cellphone,' he said. 'Did you know?' He slipped a metal plate sideways across the middle of Isidore and a small square of keys was revealed.

'Do I get the headset, too?' Andy asked. 'The virtual reality? He showed me how to work it.'

'Gwendal might come back,' I said. 'You can't just take his things.'

Andy gave me an offended look but Mum told us that, as far as she was concerned, Andy could have every bit of equipment in Gwendal's room. He had chosen to live with someone who could provide him with anything he wanted, so why shouldn't we use what he'd decided he didn't need.

'I don't think it was quite like that,' Dad murmured.

No more was said on the subject of Gwendal's possessions, and I knew that I would probably be making as much use of them as Andy.

'I could try and contact him,' Andy offered. 'If I can find a code somewhere on Isidore, perhaps I could reach him. I'll have a go.'

Andy spent the rest of Sunday in Gwendal's room. I don't know if he was playing or working, but when I looked in on him, just before I went to bed, he was staring at the computer screen. 'I've found a clue,' he said. 'Some sort of rhyme. I'd been testing Isidore to see if he could help and I used the word – well, "seek" actually, and this appeared on the screen.'

I looked over Andy's shoulder.

'WHICH IS BEST? EAST OR WEST?'

'Must be west,' said Andy. 'It rhymes with best.'

The next part read, 'WHICH DO YOU KISS? NORTH OR SOUTH?'

'Must be south because it rhymes with mouth,' said Andy, 'you kiss with a mouth, don't you?'

'So far so good, but what about the next bit?'

This was the strange sort of poem, but the way it was set out gave us a few clues. The words in the middle of each line began with capital letters, breaking the rules of grammar as I knew it.

First you must Find
The Grave of our people;

> In Places of splendour
> They were killed, they were Burned
> With fire in the Churches
> With Battle-axe and sword.

'Perhaps,' said Andy, who'd been pondering this puzzle far longer than I had, 'perhaps, we take the first letter from the first word with a capital letter, like the F in find, and then the second letter in the next, like the R in Grave, and so on . . .'

'Excluding the words at the beginning of each line, which automatically have a capital letter,' I said.

It didn't take us long, staring at the poem, to end up with this:

> First you must *F*ind
> The G*r*ave of our people;
> In Pl*a*ces of splendour,
> They were killed, they were Bur*n*ed
> With fire in the Chur*c*hes
> With Battl*e*-axe and sword.

At the same time we both shouted, 'FRANCE!'

'What are you doing?' Polly looked in sleepily.

'We've found out where Gwendal's gone,' I told her.

'We think we have,' added Andy. 'We don't know for sure. I'm going to show the poem to Dad. It must mean something more than just a few words strung together.'

Andy printed out every sentence of the strange message together with our conclusions, and we ran down to the sitting-room. Polly followed us, yawning but determined not to be left out.

Dad was wearing his half-moon spectacles to read the paper, and I thought he looked sad and tired.

'Look!' Andy presented his print-out, laying it over the article Dad was reading. Dad began to brush the paper away impatiently, but Andy said, 'We think it's the clue, Gwendal found about his . . . his what do we call him? Sponsor? It could be where he's gone.'

Dad regarded the print-out, warily at first and then with interest, 'South – West – France – yes,' he agreed. 'I think you're right.'

'But the poem,' I sat on the arm of his chair. 'What does it mean?'

'It's violent, that's for sure. Sounds like some sort of inquisition.' Milo held it closer, as though to make up for some defect in his spectacles.

'Let me see.' Mum took the paper. 'Cathars,' she announced. 'It must be about the Cathars – a heretical sect in the Middle Ages. They were burned to death by the crusaders because they disobeyed the Pope. Some escaped to their castles in the mountains, the Pyrenees, but they were rooted out until only one safe place was left – Montségur – secure mountain. In the end that fell too, and the Cathars were finished.'

'Mary, you've been hiding your light,' Dad beamed at her.

'It's not so difficult,' she confessed. 'I've been selling trips to tourists in that region for years. Bicycle trips, usually. They call it the Cathar Trail. It's supposed to be very beautiful. But it's a huge mountainous region. Easy to hide in, almost impossible to search. Wherever would you begin?'

'Wait,' said Andy. 'If we have a telephone code for that region, then all we need is another number. I'm sure Isidore can help.' Andy was proving to be quite clever after all. 'I'll keep trying,' he said.

'Tomorrow,' Mum told him. 'After school.'

When we went upstairs again I felt the heavy atmosphere in the house had lifted. Gwendal had been with us only a few weeks, and most of that time he had spent in his room. I had been told he was my brother, and then discovered that he was not. But my mind had erased that last instruction. I missed Gwendal and it raised my spirits to know where he might have gone.

'Well done, Andy,' I murmured.

I hadn't seen him look so pleased with himself for ages. 'It wasn't so hard,' he said, grinning.

Before I went to bed I slipped into Gwendal's room and put on the virtual reality suit. I couldn't remember the key to finding the people on the beach, so I asked Isidore for help. He seemed strangely remote, almost exhausted. 'Please, Isidore,' I begged. 'Do this for Gwendal, for Gwendal and me.'

Very slowly something began to happen. I found myself looking down on to a wooded plateau that fell sharply into nowhere. From the chasm beyond, a range of snow-capped mountains rose into a moonlit sky. White and desolate, they didn't seem to hold a single living thing. I could feel the cold, cold air touching my face and even catching at my lungs, and all at once I knew that he was seeing this, that he was there, on that cold mountain, safe for sure, but even lonelier than before.

I switched off the suit and removed the helmet. Isidore stood quietly blinking at me.

'Thank you for that,' I said, and then I picked him up and took him to my room. I didn't want him to be alone.

We all left the house together next morning. Mum was already at her desk in another part of town. We had just reached the gate when a person with a large camera leapt in front of us. I must say these paparazzi certainly move. One minute the pavement was deserted; the next it was full of two intrusive people. The man held the camera, the woman was tall and masculine-looking, with cropped hair and a long coat.

'Milo McCool! You're one of the Dark Knights, I believe!' She smiled unconvincingly.

Milo stood frowning. He hadn't been a Dark Knight for ten years.

'Where's the fourth child?' asked the cameraman. 'We were told there were four.'

'Oh, no!' Milo closed his eyes. He looked as if he were in pain. 'This is too much. My younger son is . . . not well. He's a very frail boy. He's . . .' Dad's eyes were now quite green. Luckily only we knew what this meant.

'What is it exactly?' the woman said suspiciously. 'An illness?'

Dad passed a hand over his face. He looked extremely distressed. 'As if life isn't bad enough without people like you being sent to torment us,' he groaned.

The reporter frowned. She was obviously in two minds, and then Polly tipped the balance. Pressing her face into Dad's sleeve, she began to cry.

Dad glared at the woman. 'He's autistic. And I'm going to make sure this intrusion never happens again.' He put his hand on the camera that the man had begun to flash. 'I shall report you to the Press Complaints Commission.'

'I'm sorry,' the woman tugged the cameraman's sleeve, and retreated a little. 'Please,' she said. 'My editor sent me. I'm only doing my job. We're doing a series on people who've fallen out of the limelight, as it were.'

'Forget the child. Perhaps you'd like to tell us a little about yourself, Milo,' the camera-man asked in a rather over-familiar tone. 'Tell us what you've been doing with yourself since the demise of *The Dark Knights*?'

'*Your* demise will occur on a dark night very soon if you don't watch it,' Dad said menacingly. 'It's none of your business and now you can just . . .' and he swore horribly, so horribly that Polly, distressed as she was, gave a shocked gasp.

It had the desired effect. The reporter and her crew walked away briskly. Without looking back they climbed into a car parked halfway down the road, and drove off.

'D'you think Nathan Culfire had something to do with that?' I asked Dad.

'Very likely,' he said grimly. 'The last bite of a wolf that knows his game is up!' He suddenly laughed and we all joined in, giggling helplessly until people began to stare at us.

And then Polly said. 'Gwendal isn't autistic, is he? I know what autistic is. We had one at school, but he didn't stay. He didn't like the teachers. I liked him, though. He was handsome.'

Milo sighed. 'Perhaps, for now, we could say Gwendal

was autistic,' he said. 'It would explain his absence.' He looked round at us. 'How about it?'

'It's OK with me,' said Andy. I nodded, and yet it didn't seem right that you couldn't tell the truth about someone without their lives being ruined.

We parted at the end of the road. Andy and I crossed at the traffic lights while Dad and Polly turned the corner. As they walked away I heard Polly say, 'You used that word, Dad. The one that costs a pound.'

Dad groaned and I knew Polly had recovered.

That evening Andy missed a football practice, he was so keen to continue his quest for Gwendal, or more precisely to work with Isidore. He was in Gwendal's room for hours, and when he finally came out his eyes were pink and shrivelled from staring at the monitor.

'No luck,' he said. 'I found numbers all right, but none of them is a code that will connect with the French number.'

'I think he'll tell us when he wants to,' I said.

I took Andy's place at the keyboard. For a while I searched for codes and played with the keys. Isidore seemed to be watching me. At length I connected him to the virtual reality suit and stepped into it. I pulled on the helmet and when I had adjusted to the dark weightless sensation, I said, 'Where is he? Show me, Isidore.'

This time Isidore didn't hesitate. The darkness of the headset was suddenly pervaded by a brilliant light. I had to close my eyes against the glare and when I opened them a moonlit snowfield lay before me. Beyond the snowfield, the now familiar mountains lifted their gaunt peaks at the stars. Such a beautiful yet barren place.

'Gwendal?' I heard my voice call. 'Are you there? Can you hear me?'

I found myself turning. Now I was looking into a room, if you could call it that. The walls were grey stone, the ceiling vaulted by wide oak beams, and a fire burned in a huge grate. I looked down and found my feet planted on a blood-red rug patterned with geometric shapes in black and gold. I moved across this mossy surface and stood before a bed; a four-poster with heavy brocade curtains.

There was no trace of Gwendal in this room, no possessions that I could see. But what had there ever been? A silver case and stark, pressed clothes. And a small robot that he'd left behind.

I turned again and saw a tall door set in a stone arch. Next to the door the contrast began. A whole wall of monitors, several keyboards and panel upon panel of coloured winking digits. Some of the monitors were blank, but others showed changing scenes: mountain peaks, a vast grey stone hall, the ocean, a library stacked floor to ceiling with large gold-tooled books, a winding track through the snow that led, eventually, to the high blank walls of a castle. And there, tucked into the lowest corner of the wall, was Gwendal's room in London, with some-one standing very still in a silver suit and helmet.

'Me!' I said. I waved, tentatively, and Laura in the monitor waved too. It was rather alarming, seeing an image of myself transported maybe a thousand miles away, at the very same instant as I was taking a breath. How was it achieved?

I searched the wall for a camera of some sort and in

the centre of the instrument panels I saw a desk. On the desk stood Isidore, or rather Isidore's twin, because this version had blue eyes.

'Isidore,' I breathed.

'Isambard,' said Isidore. 'My partner.'

'Of course,' I murmured. Isidore was, among many things, a camera. His two green eyes were lenses and even while he was engaged in other tasks, he was constantly relaying images across the sea to Isambard.

'But where are you, Gwendal?' I begged. 'It's no use just to know you're in a mountain castle. I want to talk to you. I want to know how things are out there. I want to know who the "Other" is.'

I felt a hand on my arm. A hand I knew? Or had I somehow flown across the sea?

2
Message from a stranger

The high stone walls began to fade, the monitors vanished and I was floating in the dark.

Someone lifted the headset away and I found myself looking into Milo's anxious face. He'd disconnected me from Isidore.

'Laura, you ought to be in bed,' he said. 'I'm not sure this game's a good idea.'

'It isn't a game,' I told him. 'I've been in Gwendal's room, his other room. I've seen where he sleeps. We're so close.'

Milo sat on the bed. 'He knows where *we* are. He has only to pick up a phone.'

I stepped out of the suit. 'Perhaps he can't. You said you were going to find him, Dad. I thought this was important to you.'

'I want to, Laura, of course I do, more than anything. But . . .' he hesitated, sighed, ran his fingers through his hair, 'let's give it a rest for a while.'

Mum had got to him, of course. No one else could have persuaded Milo to give up so easily. Mum thought Gwendal was too dangerous. She couldn't put the rest of us at risk.

'Wouldn't you even like to see his room?' I asked.

Dad smiled and said, 'Well, I can't get into the suit, that's for sure. But give me the headset and we'll see if it works for me.'

The helmet was a tight fit, but when I'd squeezed it over Milo's head, I connected it to Isidore and said, 'Gwendal! Gwendal's room, Isidore. Please!'

Milo was very still. Only his fingers moved, clenching and relaxing. I didn't know if Isidore was doing what I'd asked, but Milo certainly seemed to be watching something. At last he raised his hand and I switched off the headset. He struggled out of it and sat blinking at me for a moment, as though he were in shock.

'What did you see?' I asked.

'Gwendal,' he told me. 'He was asleep.' He sat staring into space for a moment, before saying, 'As you should be. Come on, Laura.'

We left Gwendal's room together and found Mum standing on the landing. She appeared to have been watching the door. For some reason I felt like a conspirator, but I couldn't help saying, 'We've found the place, Mum. I saw his room, and Dad saw him sleeping.'

'We still don't know where he is, though,' Dad said quickly.

'Laura, it's very late.' Mum looked at Dad as she spoke. 'You should be in bed.'

It was as if we hadn't even mentioned Gwendal. But her expression betrayed her and for the first time I realised she'd had to harden her heart. She had always been afraid of losing him.

A week passed, and if the first day was hardly normal, the seventh was almost the same as all the days that had passed before we ever knew about Gwendal. Andy spent less and less time with Isidore, until by Saturday football had entirely won him back again.

Mind you, Andy did have to make one agonizing decision. When he came home on Saturday he had to chose between Snow and Flake. One of them must go, Mum said. We couldn't have baby rats appearing at monthly intervals. He was allowed to keep one ratlet, as long as it was the same sex as the parent he chose.

When Andy disappeared into his room to make his terrible choice, he was covered in rats, literally. They clung to his shoulders, hung from his sleeves, poked out of pockets and nestled in his neck.

I thought Mum's ultimatum was draconian. 'Why can't one of them have an operation?' I asked her. 'Like the cat did?'

'It didn't save Alfie,' Polly murmured.

'That's beside the point,' I argued. 'Mum, I know rats can be operated on.'

'It's a waste of money.' Her voice was like polar ice.

When Andy reappeared I could see that he'd been crying. He handed Mum a box and said, 'Take them.' Then he turned away very quickly and when I asked which one he'd chosen to keep, he wouldn't tell me. He just rushed upstairs again.

'Poor Andy,' Polly remarked. 'I wouldn't like to make a decision like that.'

We peeped in the box before Mum took them off to the pet shop. 'Flake!' I said. 'He's given Flake away.'

'She was his favourite,' Polly whispered, glancing at Mum. And I sensed a slight weakening in the glue that had always bound Polly so closely to our mother.

When Mum had gone Polly said, 'We haven't been terrorized once this week, not by newspaper ladies, or rollerbladers, or even smelly Culfire. Maybe it *is* better without Gwendal.'

I almost shouted at her, but I stopped myself because I couldn't deny it was true, and I realized she had only meant that our lives were easier.

'Safer,' I said. 'Not better.'

'OK. Safer,' she agreed.

On Monday morning, just before we left for school, something extraordinary happened. Milo got a job. A real one. We heard him talking on the phone while we were having breakfast. His voice went tight and quite high for him.

'Are you sure?' we heard him say. 'Without an audition? When? Hugh this is . . . it's –. What can I say? Thanks, Hugh!' (Hugh Simmonds is Dad's agent.)

Dad leapt into the kitchen, spread his arms and cried, 'Milo's got a job, kids!'

I have to confess our congratulations were a bit feeble. For my part I was wondering what sort of job it was. Milo hadn't worked within my living memory.

Andy asked, 'What kind of job is it, Dad?'

'They want my voice,' Milo told us, 'for a commercial. A long one. A prestigious one. Prime time.'

'Cars?' said Andy.

'How did you guess?' Milo beamed. 'Come on, be a bit more enthusiastic. It's money, kiddoes!'

'Oh money!' said Polly. 'How much?'

'A lot.'

'Hooray, for Dad,' I cheered.

So when we left the house we were a merry crew. Christmas was coming and Dad would have money. We couldn't help applying this news to ourselves. Polly skipped, Andy whistled and I swung my bag. And then Polly, stopping dead in the middle of the pavement, said, 'But who's going to take me to school?'

'I will,' I said, not even glancing at Andy. 'And I'll bring you home.' I knew, somehow, that the wolves had left with Gwendal.

I was surprised when Andy murmured, 'I will too.'

'There'll be no need,' Milo told us. 'It doesn't take long to record a few sentences. I'll be back before the end of school, I'm sure.'

'And your voice will be in every household in the land,' sang Polly.

'Every household with a TV on the right channel,' said pragmatic Andy.

And so it was.

The commercial came on a week before Christmas, and Milo's voice, smooth as silk and rich as dark chocolate, swam into households up and down the country.

We sat together in the living-room and watched the first one. It was a brilliant commercial: a long silvery car slides through a forest of snowy trees, crosses a frozen lake, sails through the sky, climbs a mountain and lands 'whoosh' beside an ornate city fountain. And in the background, Milo's voice explains, describes and seduces.

'Wow!' said Andy. 'I'd buy that.'

'Wonderful,' cried Mum, clapping her hands. 'You'll get more work after this, Milo. I know it.'

And he did. Next morning he had two offers. Another commercial and a small but important part in a flashy new drama.

I wanted to know if Dad would have to do any stunts. He admitted that he wouldn't this time. 'You wait, though,' he said. 'The parts will come. Soon I'll be leaping off a bridge again.'

Mum gave him a look. I'm not sure what it meant.

Dad's success worked like a charm on Polly's friend Jessica. The pirate episode was conveniently forgotten and it was all, 'Can Polly come and play?', 'Can Polly come and stay?'

Polly could and would.

'You shouldn't give in so easily,' I told Polly. 'Jessica was pretty mean.'

But Polly was eager to forgive.

Andy had always been popular at school, now he was bombarded with offers. He accepted the skiing holiday with Gary Allen and his family. They would be setting off two days after Christmas.

Life didn't change at all for me. No offers came. If anything the girls in my class seemed to resent my father's success. I hadn't had a real friend for ages, since the Drinkwater-Art teacher reference. I don't know why. Mum told me I didn't make enough of an effort. I had two attributes: curiosity and imagination. You'd have thought at least one of these would have helped to acquire a few friends. I was always willing to listen to problems. But perhaps the advice I gave wasn't what was required.

'We'll go somewhere, just the two of us, shall we?' Dad said. We were sitting in the kitchen sharing a pot of tea. Everyone else was out.

'You'll be busy,' I said. 'Your new part.'

'Rehearsals don't start for another two weeks,' Milo told me. 'We'll have plenty of time.' A touch of astonishment crept into his smile.

I found myself asking, 'How has it happened, Dad? I mean, why now, after all this time?'

He looked at me and I answered for him, 'Do you think it's Gwendal? Somewhere, out there, persuading someone rich and powerful, who owns satellites and newspapers and factories and castles?'

'One should never underestimate power,' Milo said, and I could see that it worried him to think someone he didn't know was manipulating his life, even if it was all very positive. For him, the mystery of his benefactor lay like a shadow over his good fortune.

'Do you remember the king who ruled the stars in *The Little Prince*?' I said.

'And the businessman who owned them,' Milo added.

'The businessman who had never smelled a flower or loved anyone.'

There was a moment of silence before Milo said, 'I don't think he is like that. I'm sure he loves Gwendal.'

'Are you?' I asked. 'Are you sure?'

'How can we bear to imagine anything else?'

'You said you were going to find him,' I reminded him.

'I will,' he said.

I couldn't see how. He hadn't been making much of an effort just lately.

Mum came in, humming. Among the food bags she carried were several exotic-looking packages. She stacked them in a corner of the kitchen. Christmas was coming.

'I wish we could send Gwendal something,' I murmured.

'So do I,' Mum said, 'but we can't. And he probably has everything he wants.'

'Just a card to show we were thinking of him,' I went on.

Mum and Dad looked at me, both tight-lipped and solemn, and Mum said, 'Yes, it would be nice.'

We had a good Christmas, I can't deny it. Milo's commercial paid well. So we all received the gifts we dreamed of. Polly's bear was almost as big as she was; an old-fashioned dark brown bear with a hump on his back and real-looking fur. Andy had a computer and I got a sound system. Although we had wanted these things I was a little surprised, seeing that there were perfectly good versions in Gwendal's abandoned room.

'You should have your own,' Dad told us. If he meant that Gwendal might one day return, he didn't say it.

Mary and Milo gave each other clothes and jewellery. They sat in front of the fire on Christmas night, toasting each other with champagne. Mary wore shiny gold and Milo a wine-coloured velvet jacket. The tallest tree we'd ever had sparkled in a corner, and our new possessions and glittery paper were scattered around the room like items in Aladdin's cave.

Lancelot was part of the scene, of course, and Andy's rats (he called the new one Drift) had been allowed in to share the mince pies. Somehow all the good cheer made

Gwendal's absence seem like a terrible void. Wherever I looked there was a shadowy fault where he should have been and when Mum held up the champagne bottle, asking if I'd like a glass, I couldn't help saying, 'How can we celebrate when someone's lost. Someone who may not be having a good time at all?'

Everyone looked at me. I couldn't read their expressions but I knew they weren't exactly happy about what I'd said. I didn't want to spoil things for them, I really didn't, but once I'd started I couldn't stop. 'If it wasn't for Gwendal we wouldn't be here,' I told them. 'We wouldn't be in this house, we wouldn't be enjoying these expensive things. But you're all behaving like he's a blank, avoiding his name like a hole in the road. We could have sent cards to the clinic, they know where he is.'

'They don't,' Milo said quietly.

'What?' I stared at him, disbelieving.

'They don't know where he is. They weren't allowed to know,' Milo told me.

'But we can see where he is,' I cried. 'We can see his room, the view from his window, the place where he lives. How can it be that no one can reach him, even with a message?'

'They have to wait,' Dad said, 'for his . . . the sponsor to contact them.'

From the arms of her new bear, Polly asked, 'What *is* wrong with Gwendal?'

'Nothing,' I said. 'There's absolutely nothing wrong with Gwendal. It's us. All of us. We're what's wrong.'

I left my family looking awkward and distressed, but I didn't care. I went up to Gwendal's room and, seeing

Isidore, picked him up. I felt his smooth chrome head with my cupped hand, and with my fingertips touched his green glass eyes, his unlikely nose and the soft mesh of his microphone mouth. I slid my hand across the neat row of silver keys, and laid him cold and smooth against my cheek.

'Take me there, Isidore,' I said. 'Take me to Gwendal.' I stood the little robot on Gwendal's desk and pulled on the silver suit and helmet.

In the darkness of the helmet I repeated my request, 'Take me to Gwendal.'

And then I was moving through the air. I closed my eyes against the motion sickness that suddenly overwhelmed me, and when I opened them again I had come to rest.

I was in a vast stone-flagged hall. Before me gleamed a long, polished table set for dinner. Candles flickered in tall silver candlesticks, there were gold-painted bowls of vegetables, silver dishes of carved meat, a jug of wine and sparkling glass goblets. But the plates, one at the head of the table and one either side of it, were empty and the carved high-backed chairs unoccupied.

I was taken round the table and through an open door. Treading the smooth floor of a narrow passage, I approached another door. This one was arched at the top and very ancient-looking. Someone opened this door and it blew back, thumping the stone wall behind it.

I paused on the threshold of the snowfield I had seen before. I felt steps descending beneath me, and if I hadn't been so buoyant I'm sure I would have slipped and fallen. I could hear the rasp of feet pressing into the snow, matching my own hesitant steps. Afraid of losing myself I turned to look back and saw that a tall, desolate castle grew out of the mountain behind me. It was hardly a building, but more a rock that had accidently acquired the contours of a castle. The awful loneliness it conveyed made me shiver.

The sigh of an icy wind turned into a howl and I swung round, battered like a scarecrow. The air suddenly filled with flying ice that dragged and pushed me forward. I knew that somewhere at the edge of the snowfield there was a chasm that fell into nowhere, and I began to be afraid that I was being pulled towards it.

The moon, torn by ragged clouds, began to lose its brilliance. Shadow raced across the snow and my heart thumped violently. I told myself it was an illusion, virtual reality, a game, that I could be at home in an instant if I wanted, but there was something so real and deadly about this journey it was hard not to believe in it.

Through the mist of flying ice I glimpsed the mountains that rose beyond the chasm. I could see the edge of the plateau now, the fatal line of snow that fell maybe a thousand feet. And then I saw him. He was wearing his black anorak and he was standing on the rim of the chasm. He seemed so small in that vast white wilderness. The void that always followed him was magnified a hundred times.

'Gwenda-l!' I called. 'Gwendal! It's me, Laura!'

Could he hear me? He turned slowly. Could he see me?

'Gwendal!' I called again. I tried to run but found myself rooted in the snow.

He took a step towards me and then stopped. One of his feet seemed poised to slip into nowhere.

'Be careful!' I cried. 'Gwendal!' I stretched out my hands and gradually he lifted his own, as if to hold on to me.

And then the moonlight was gone, and so was Gwendal. I waited a moment but our link had been broken. I was left in the dark with only the floating after-image of a boy lifting his hand.

As I stepped out of the suit, the robot clicked twice and then the light behind his green eyes went out.

'A lot of use, you are!' I muttered. I was about to leave the room when I suddenly regretted what I'd said. 'I'm sorry,' I murmured. 'I suppose you've done as much as you can. Thank you, anyway.'

I opened the door and walked straight into Mum. She'd been listening, that was obvious. I knew what she was going to say, so I forestalled her with a grin and said, 'I'm sorry, Mum. I just couldn't help thinking about him. You made me feel like his sister, and I can't stop feeling like one just because he's gone.'

'You've got to try,' she said. 'We've all managed, why should you be the exception?'

I couldn't answer that. 'I saw him,' I told her. 'I think he'll try to contact us soon. Oh, Mum, please look happy!'

'You almost spoiled Christmas,' she said impassively.

'Almost . . . but not quite,' I said.

'No, not quite.' She walked away from me.

We never recaptured the spirit of Christmas again that year, although I don't think Polly and Andy even noticed. They were very busy and excited about their forthcoming holidays. Andy spent hours on the phone to Gary, discussing winter sports, while Polly packed and re-packed her clothes for her stay with Jessica. I spent most of my time listening for Isidore's bleep. Now and again I looked in Gwendal's room, hoping for a message. But nothing appeared.

In two days my brother and sister had gone. Mum went back to work and Dad and I tried to plan a New Year's Eve for three.

We were sitting in the kitchen, making lists, when the phone rang. Dad leapt up. He'd been expecting a call from his agent, but his voice, when he spoke at last, was hoarse with shock.

'What?' he exclaimed.

I looked into the hall. Dad was glaring into space. 'Yes!' he said. 'Yes, of course. Laura's been waiting. She looks in every day. Yes. Hold on. I'll get a pen.' He felt in his pockets and shook his head.

I rushed back to the kitchen, grabbed a pencil and a grubby piece of paper, ran and put them on the table beside Dad.

He gave me an anxious smile and began to talk aloud as he took down the message.

'Urgent . . . Toulouse . . . tickets, Heathrow. Terminal 2 . . . red Trekker . . . number . . . Yes . . . OK . . . keys . . . special delivery. No, it's not a problem. I'll be here. The children are away,' he looked at me and shrugged, 'at least two of them are. I'll bring this one with me.'

'Yes!' I whispered. 'Yes, yes, yes!'

Milo replaced the receiver.

'What is it, Dad? What's happened?' I begged.

'They've been trying to reach us,' he said grimly, 'but someone has shut down the computer and every other damn thing in Gwendal's room.'

We stared at each other.

'Mum,' I said. 'But it's my fault. I never thought to check.'

'It isn't your fault, Laura,' he said.

'But who has been trying to reach us?'

'The man I've always wanted to meet. He's very sure of himself. The tickets are at Heathrow already. I think he expected Mary, but,' he grinned at me, 'I don't think she'll want to go just now. I'm sure he'll accept you instead. We fly to Toulouse at midday tomorrow. There'll be a red Trekker waiting outside the airport. The keys will arrive in the morning by special messenger.'

I couldn't take it all in. I kept running over the details as though it were an adventure about to happen to someone in a story, not me, Laura McCool, who never went anywhere.

'Why d'you think he wants to see you?' I said at last. 'Why now?'

Milo's eyes were troubled, and yet he looked hopeful. 'Who knows?' he said.

It wasn't difficult to guess. Something had happened to Gwendal.

3
Hiding-place

We forgot New Year's Eve. I brushed aside the scraps of lists and plans, and Dad got out the atlas.

'Toulouse,' he said, flicking the pages until he found France.

'And if it has something to do with the clues on Gwendal's computer, then south,' I said. 'Remember it had to rhyme with mouth.' I was looking at the Pyrenees, even before Dad's finger began to trace a line from Toulouse.

'Of course,' he said. 'The Cathar trail goes into the Pyrenees.'

'Are we really going *there*?' I exclaimed.

'Perhaps not, but somewhere near. Tomorrow we'll find out, Lo!' He gave me a hug.

For a moment my dad looked as he must have twenty years ago, when he was still a carefree actor. And then we heard Mary's key in the lock and remembered New Year's Eve.

Dad didn't have time to organize his phrases. There we were with a map of France open on the table; he had to explain.

'Mary, love,' he waltzed towards her and took her bags and briefcase.

Mum smiled briefly and sat down. 'What's all this, then?' she said, twisting her head to get a better view of the map.

'France,' My voice sounded guilty, though I hadn't meant it to.

'Ah, France.' Mum looked suspicious.

'We've heard from Gwendal,' Dad told her cheerfully. 'At last. We'll be seeing him.'

'Gwendal?' she said.

'Gwendal, yes,' Dad said slowly. 'But more than that; I've had a message from the man himself. The sponsor. Still don't know his name, though.'

'We would have had it sooner,' I said accusingly. Dad shot me a warning glance but I couldn't stop. 'Everything in Gwendal's room had been turned off.'

'I'm sorry, I just thought . . .' Mum looked guilty. 'I gather you'll be travelling very soon, then.' She nodded at the map and looked at Milo. 'When?'

'Tomorrow,' Dad said. 'I'm sorry, Mary. It's too soon, isn't it?'

'There are two tickets, Mum,' I said. 'D'you want to go?'

She hardly had to glance at my face to guess my anxious thoughts. 'Of course not. You can't stay here alone, Laura. Besides, I'm far too busy.'

'But New Year's Eve?' I murmured.

'They're having a bit of a "do" at the office,' she said.

I'm not sure that I believed her, but I tried not to think about what she might feel. To be honest, I think she rather liked the idea of having the house to herself after the chaos of the last few weeks.

She helped me to pack, finding extra-thick socks and jumpers. It might be southern France, she said, but it was going to be cold in the mountains, especially in midwinter.

As promised, the mysterious key arrived at seven o'clock next morning. Mum was already up, cooking us a huge breakfast. She seemed not at all put out by Gwendal's sudden re-emergence in our lives. Perhaps all along she had suspected it would happen. Now that he was safe she could allow herself to think about him without the distress that Culfire had caused.

My stomach was churning and I could hardly eat a thing. I couldn't look on the trip as a holiday, but more as a sort of quest. After all, we didn't know why Dad had been summoned. Some terrible crisis could have occurred.

If the same thought had crossed Dad's mind he never let on. He ate every scrap of Mary's enormous meal, and the taxi he had ordered arrived just as he was swallowing his third cup of coffee.

We grabbed our rucksacks, and then we were on the foggy doorstep while Mum and Dad rocked together in the deepest hug I'd seen for a long time. It warmed my soul.

I don't remember much about the journey. There was the usual delay at Heathrow, but it was still light when we reached Toulouse. The big red Trekker was in the car park, exactly where the message said it would be. The key turned in the lock and we were in.

A map was in the driving seat, as promised, but it was the handwritten envelope that caught our attention. 'For

Milo McCool'. The writing slanted imperiously, in long thick strokes. Dad picked it up but wouldn't open it until we were both sitting inside.

It could have been anyone's hand: a secretary, an assistant, the general factotum . . . and yet I knew it was *his*. I think Milo did too. He stared at the writing for a moment, turned the envelope over in his hand, stared again, then ripped it open. He withdrew a sheet of thick cream-coloured paper. The message was written in the same bold hand.

> Welcome, Mr McCool – and perhaps, Mrs Mc Cool.
>
> You have now reached Toulouse. I'm afraid there is a long drive ahead of you. There was no other way to do this. On the map I have marked your route to Saint-Luc in red ink. You will see that it is not straightforward. You must drive another 150 kilometres south into the Pyrenees. The terrain is rough and it will take you several hours. I have, therefore, arranged for you to take a meal at the gîte marked on your map. Gîte Marguerite. They are expecting you. The worst part of your journey will follow. We await you here, at Fort Saint-Luc.
>
> *Bonne chance*,
>
> Jean Tisseyre

Milo gave a low whistle. 'So that's who it is. I would never have guessed.'

'Who is he, Dad?' I'd never heard the name before.

'A billionaire who's clawed his fortune from eating up

companies. He owns a part of anything you can name: mobile phones, airlines, media companies, restaurants, records, computers. Jean Tisseyre's got a slice of every-thing. He's quite ruthless.'

'Wow! And he's . . . Gwendal? Or what Gwendal might be?' It seemed so unlikely. I suddenly realized how little I really knew of Gwendal.

Although there had been a weak apology in the letter, it didn't appear to be sincere. The words had been written by someone whose commands were never questioned.

'He doesn't sound particularly grateful,' I muttered.

'It's in English,' Dad pointed out. 'That shows consideration.'

'There's nothing about Gwendal in the letter,' I said. 'Monsieur Tisseyre still doesn't say why he wants you here.'

'We'll have to be patient.' Dad put the map in my lap and dialled our number on his mobile.

Mum answered immediately. She must have been waiting for the call. Milo described our journey briefly and then the letter. I heard Mum say, 'D'you think we have the real name at last?'

'Who knows?' Dad said. 'The man probably has a thousand aliases.'

'Take care, Milo,' said Mum's faraway voice. 'And give Gwendal my love.'

'Of course. Here's Laura!'

Mum and I spoke briefly, blew kisses into the receiver and then she was gone. Our last link with the real world.

Dad started the engine, and the big Trekker purred through the car park and out on to the main road.

Milo had a gift. He always knew where he was going.

So map-reading wasn't a priority for me. I could dream, not really taking in the scenery until we approached the foothills. Then I sat up and just gazed. The sun was descending and the snow-clad mountains swam on the horizon like the vision of another world. It was only then that I became aware how remote we were from everything we knew.

A few more kilometres and the light had left the sky. Now we had only the road ahead to watch, and the odd glitter of a distant village. I fell asleep and didn't wake until Milo shook my shoulder, saying, 'We're here, Laura! Time to eat!'

For a moment I thought we had reached Fort Saint-Luc, but we were at the gîte where a meal was waiting for us.

Monsieur Loué was a square, almost silent, man. His smile was suspicious and rather hesitant. Madame, on the other hand, was wiry and chatty. She spoke good English and had probably been quite beautiful, once. She loved visitors, she told us. In summer the gîte was always full. 'Bicyclists,' she explained. 'They come this way to visit the Cathar castles.'

'Do you know Fort Saint-Luc?' Dad asked.

'I know it but have never entered,' she said mysteriously.

Madame was a great cook. We ate soup and fish and mounds of local cheese and crusty bread. Dad even let me polish off a glass of red wine, seeing as it was from a local vineyard. I could tell that he longed to down a whole bottle but didn't dare because of the driving ahead. This was to be the most hazardous part of our journey.

We dragged ourselves away from the cosy kitchen, pulled on our winter gear again and stepped out into the dark. The temperature had dropped several degrees and the icy path crunched under our feet.

'Come again,' called Madame Loué, 'and please take care. It will not snow, I think, but the ground is icy and very dangerous. Drive slowly, slowly, slowly.'

Dad answered that he would. We said our goodbyes and the Trekker rumbled out on to the silent road. If you could call it a road. It looked hardly more than a track to me.

Dad had to consult the map in earnest now. Some of the tracks that intersected ours were not marked at all. Monsieur Tisseyre's red route looped and swung in a complex pattern as it neared the village of Saint-Luc. Several times we came to a halt, Dad quietly cursing his luck and the local geography. He would peer at the map, push his specs further up his nose, and then roar off again. I was no help at all.

We bumped along narrow lanes where the cliffs were so close on either side, they almost formed a tunnel. We passed over an ancient bridge with crumbling stone walls, and then, suddenly, a dense blanket of trees engulfed us.

'Ah,' said Milo, surprisingly pleased. 'I know where we are.'

Another mile and the trees thinned. We could see lights ahead and Milo murmured, 'This must be it. Saint-Luc. Nearly there, Lo.' He began to sing as we approached the village, and I found myself joining in, my voice high and silly with relief. How glad I was that Dad was beside me. In that dark and utterly foreign place, I wouldn't have wished for anyone else. And then I heard the wolf.

I grabbed Milo's arm and almost at the same time, something leapt on to the road in front of us. Not a wolf: a figure in a long hooded coat. It stood there, waving its arms across its body and then out again, making the shape of a crucifix. Behind the figure the luminous eyes of an animal swam from side to side as the creature rushed howling about the path.

Dad pulled up. He had no choice. The figure approached and we held our breaths.

'What the hell?' Dad muttered.

The hood nodded at us; and then a fist came out of a long grey sleeve and knocked on Milo's window. He gripped the steering wheel and stared grimly ahead.

'Please, Monsieur,' said a muffled voice. 'Please! I speak with you?' It sounded reasonable.

Milo opened the window a fraction and the voice became clearer. 'Monsieur McCool?'

'Yes,' Dad grunted.

'*Ah, bien*! Monsieur Tisseyre tell me, wait for you here. You must leave the car, Monsieur, and walk now.'

'What?' Milo said angrily. 'It's freezing. My daughter's with me – she's a child.'

'Huh!' I muttered.

'I'm sorry, Monsieur. It's necessary. There was snow last night and then ice, the road is perilous.' The shadowed face waited.

Milo sat wordlessly drumming his fingers on the wheel. 'How d'you feel, Lo?' He put an arm round my shoulders.

'I'm OK,' I said. 'I could do with a walk. He seems all right. At least his voice does.'

Milo sighed. 'What do we do with the car?' he asked the hood.

'Follow, please.' The man moved in front of the car and beckoned. We followed slowly and came into a small square, surrounded by pale stone houses. The man motioned us to slow down, then turn into a rough sort of shelter beside one of the houses.

Dad shrugged. Inside the shelter he turned off the engine and murmured. 'This is it, then. End of the road, almost. Let's get our gear.'

We jumped out and emerged into the square. An icy wind swept round my head and, looking up, I saw the cliff. It rose almost sheer above the village, a dark wall of rock, so steep that even snow couldn't cling to it, though here and there, glinting in the light from the village, I could see icicles hanging from deep fissures in the rock.

'Is it up there?' I asked. 'Fort Saint-Luc?'

'Don't worry, Mademoiselle,' the stranger said. 'We go round, and there is a good path. No rock-climbing, eh?' He laughed and held out his hand, 'Gérard Bezain.'

'Milo McCool,' Dad shook the hand. 'And this is Laura.'

As Gérard turned to me, he pulled back his hood and I saw that he had black springy hair and a big smile. His eyes creased in a very friendly way and his hand was warm. I felt at ease.

'You follow me, now,' said Gérard. 'See. I have the torch.' He showed us his big flashlight. 'And Laura, you will give me your baggage, no?'

I willingly handed over my rucksack, and pulled on my woolly hat. As we walked across the square I noticed that the rest of the village, such as it was, seemed to be asleep. Only one light showed in the house where we parked the Trekker. We passed a square stone tower, and looking at the clock face at the top, I noticed it was already past midnight.

Dad took my hand but as we began to climb away from the village, the road became a narrow track and he had to fall back, so that we were walking in single file.

'The road is there, you see,' Gérard swung his torch. 'It is impossible.'

We saw, far ahead, a broad ribbon of white, where frozen snow had formed an icy slide.

'Impossible indeed. Excellent for a bobsleigh, though.' Dad chuckled and I tried to remember if the Dark Knights had ever had a snowy adventure, but I could only think of James Bond in *The Living Daylights*.

The path became steeper and more treacherous. Steps had been chipped into the rock, but being icy and uneven they were just as hard to climb as a track of slippery stones.

'Good thing we're fit, eh, Laura?' Dad muttered behind me.

I grunted. The adventurous spirit I'd started out with was beginning to flag. My legs ached, my nose was freezing and once again I was very hungry.

'In summer it is beautiful!' Gérard called out encouragingly. 'There are goats here, with their bells, and wild flowers . . . would you believe it?'

I wouldn't, but I didn't have the energy to say so.

'Tomorrow you will have the view,' he promised. 'Ah, that is something, I can tell you.'

Even Milo had given up speech. I could hear him breathing, rather heavily, below me.

Just when I thought all my limbs would drop off, the ground levelled out and I found myself in a wide snow-filled drive. A lantern hung in a vaulted stone porch, and beyond it a dark oak door began to open.

It was my first sight of him, the man who was supposedly Gwendal's other self. Bizarre, was my first thought. Time and again his image would resurface, when I was old and he was long gone. It was something I could never forget.

He was tall for an old man, and very straight. His snow white hair was still thick and he wore his long moustaches in a style I have always thought foreign and slightly dangerous. His clothes were dark and had a rich velvety appearance.

'Good evening.' Even his voice was not a disap-point-ment, bass and romantically French. Not a patch on Dad's, of course, but rather thrilling for all that. '*Merci*, Gérard!' He lifted his hand.

'*Ils sont arrivés*!' Gérard responded cheerfully. He came to the door with us and then, dropping my rucksack at my feet, he shook our hands once more. Explaining that he must not keep his wife awake any longer, he vanished into the night.

I found Jean Tisseyre staring at me. He seemed sur-prised and yet delighted. Dad quickly explained that Mum couldn't come and I was an excellent travelling companion.

'I am sure.' Monsieur Tisseyre took my hand in both of his and gazed intently at me. I noticed that his eyes were brown and had once been very dark perhaps. 'You are a good friend of Gwendal's, I think.'

'Of course, I'm his sister,' I replied.

'Of course,' he smiled. 'Come in! Come in!'

We followed him down a long paved corridor, through another tall door and into a vast hall. I immediately recognized the long table at the far end. It bore the same silver candlesticks, and the same carved high backed chairs stood at either end. No attempt had been made to plaster the rough stone walls which rose around us, up and up to vaulted beams and a round skylight that showed us the moon.

'Our *salon* – our living-room,' said Monsieur Tisseyre. I didn't tell him that I'd seen it already.

The flagged stone floor was scattered with Persian carpets. The furniture was dark, the sofas plump and leathery. The lamps on the ornately carved chests cast a rich golden glow, but best of all to me, just then, were the leaping flames in the great stone fireplace. I dropped my rucksack and made for the fire.

Milo was still gazing at the domed ceiling when our host said, 'Come,' and drew him to the fire.

From behind a curtain at the far end of the hall, a man appeared; small, swarthy and completely bald.

'This is Raoul,' said Monsieur Tisseyre. 'He is my right arm, he does everything!'

Raoul carried a tray to the low table in front of the fire. He set out cups of tea, a bottle of cognac and two tumblers.

'English tea,' said Jean Tisseyre, 'or would you like some juice?'

'English tea,' I cried. I dropped into the sofa that was as soft as it looked, and smiling Raoul handed me a gold-patterned cup.

We were told that Gwendal was probably asleep, and very soon my own eyes were closing. Raoul brought me some thick toast which I suppose I must have asked for, and I listened to Milo and Monsieur Tisseyre murmuring in low voices. They were discussing the work that had so miraculously come Dad's way in the last few weeks. I gathered it was all Gwendal's idea. Jean changed the subject without mentioning Gwendal again, and I dozed off to sleep.

I found Dad gently helping me on to my feet when I woke up, minutes or maybe hours later. And then we were following Raoul up a flight of steps and along another corridor, thickly carpeted this time.

My room was small and cosy. There were the same grey stone walls, but the ceiling was low and my bed a four-poster with heavy brocade curtains. It was all a bit too much like a dream, or a nightmare, depending which way you looked at it.

'Are you OK, then, Lo?' Dad asked, barely disguising a yawn.

'I'm fine,' I said. 'Did you find out why we're here, Dad?'

'He wouldn't discuss it tonight, or I should say this morning. I think our Monsieur Tisseyre likes to keep people guessing.'

When Dad had gone I gazed round the room,

searching for anything that Gwendal might have left to entertain me. And then I remembered that he hadn't known I was coming. Perhaps Jean had kept even Dad's visit as a surprise.

Before I got into bed, I drew aside the velvet curtain that hung over the window. The scene below shocked me wide awake. Bright moonlight showed a vista of icy mountains stretching into infinity, while below me a snowy plateau fell sharply into impenetrable darkness. This was where I had last seen Gwendal. On the edge of the plateau. Why had he been there? Had he known that I could see him? Was he trying to reach me? Tomorrow I would know.

I slept very deeply and didn't open my eyes until Dad's voice crept into my head.

'Laura, wake up! It's a wonderful morning, and we've had a breakfast call.'

'Don't go down without me, Dad,' I cried.

He waited patiently, in the passage, while I leapt into my clothes and dashed to the bathroom with my toothbrush.

We found Jean Tisseyre in his carved chair at one end of the hall table. He was reading a newspaper and drinking black coffee. No cosy kitchen breakfast, then, I thought. Where was Gwendal?

'Good morning,' Jean said. 'You are hungry.'

I wasn't sure if this was a question or a statement, but said yes anyway. So did Milo.

Like a genie, Raoul appeared with mounds of steaming food: bacon, eggs, chips and vegetables. 'English breakfast,' he announced, beaming at us.

In daylight the great hall was even more impressive. The glass-domed ceiling was filled with brilliant blue, and sunlight bounced off all the polished surfaces.

'Where's Gwendal?' I asked with my mouth full of chips.

Monsieur Tisseyre didn't look up. 'You're wondering if someone has been down to Saint-Luc to fetch my paper, no?' he said. 'I'll tell you. The paper is two days old, but still I read it.' He looked over his reading glasses and grinned beneath his exotic moustache.

'Is Gwendal up? Has he gone out?' I persisted.

Jean appeared not to hear me, but then Milo made sure the question got through. 'Jean – does Gwendal know we're here?' he asked. 'I think it's time you told us what all this is about.'

'You are right.' Jean carefully folded his newspaper, over and over into a neat rectangle. He drew his half-moon spectacles down his nose and placed them carefully on the table.

We waited.

'Milo – Laura,' Jean looked at me. 'Gwendal is not here.'

'What?' Dad dropped his fork and glared across the table. 'Where the hell is he, then?'

Jean stroked a corner of his moustache. 'I do not know.'

This really got Dad going. 'Why didn't you tell us? When did he go? Have you told the police?'

'How can I?' said Jean. 'They would ask questions that cannot be answered.'

'But why did he go?' I asked, thinking of the boy in

his black coat, standing on the brink of darkness.

'I have no idea,' Jean spread his hands. 'That is why you are here.'

4
The drowned boy

Milo McCool exploded, then. His swearing was loud and inventive. He leapt up and cursed Jean Tisseyre, the billionaire, for his negligence, his careless-ness, for being who he was, for putting Gwendal at risk, for arrogance and even stupidity. I could feel that he wanted to kick something, or jump on a table. But even Milo could see that it was not the sort of furniture you abused.

If Polly's swear box had been around it would have been too heavy to lift by the end of Dad's little session.

None of it cut any ice with Monsieur Tisseyre, however. He'd probably weathered hundreds of tantrums in his cut-throat career. He just waited until Dad's imagination had run dry, then he said, 'I agree with you,' as cool as a cucumber.

Milo stood quite still. 'You agree with me,' he stated, looking mystified.

'But, of course,' said Jean. 'I am filled with remorse. I have reproached myself a thousand times. Everything you have said aloud, Milo, I have said to myself – not perhaps in those terms precisely, but nevertheless, I expressed the same sentiments to myself, and to Raoul, who is my only confidant.'

'Why didn't you tell me the truth last night?' asked Milo in a more reasonable tone.

Jean Tisseyre sighed. 'I was afraid you would turn and go.'

'Rather unlikely in the circumstances,' Milo muttered. 'We're virtually prisoners here.'

'Not at all.' Jean gave a big French shrug. 'Anyway I did not want to alarm you. When you had slept, I thought, you would see things more . . . rationally.'

'I see.' Milo suddenly looked a bit green. Jumping about with an English breakfast inside him can't have helped. He sat down rather quickly, and said, 'I see,' again.

Someone had to start being practical, so I asked, 'How are we supposed to help?'

'You have come to know Gwendal,' Jean said. 'You must understand him better than I, much better. I'm so glad that you are here, Laura,' he gave me a warm smile. 'You can tell us how he thinks, what concerns him, why he runs, first from you, and now from me.'

'Did he tell you about Nathan Culfire?' asked Milo.

'Gwendal told me nothing. Only that he felt it was time for us to see each other. To tell the truth my heart leapt when I heard those words.'

Jean didn't look the type of person whose heart leapt. He gave the impression that he was well past joy or astonishment of any kind, and it wasn't just his age. Yet when I studied him a little more closely, I was surprised by the truthfulness in his eyes.

'I think you should know about Mr Culfire,' I said.

'Tell me,' Jean commanded.

Milo told him the facts, including the role of the

sinister skaters. I would have said more. I wanted Jean Tisseyre to see Nathan Culfire as I had seen him: his greasy fedora and his grey cloak, with his long black hair and hidden eyes; interfering, repulsive, threatening, odd.

'Do you want to tell me something, Laura?' Jean asked. 'What do you make of this Mr Culfire?'

'He's dangerous,' I said.

He nodded. 'I agree. Fanatics are not amusing. To us their causes may be laughable, but they can be ruthless and cunning. The Society for Angels has never had a real angel.'

'You know about the Society for Angels?' I exclaimed.

'Before Gwendal was . . . born,' Jean said. 'I had to know about everything that might threaten him.'

'But Gwendal isn't an angel,' I declared. 'He's just a boy. I know he began life in a different way, but he hasn't got wings, he's not perfect in any way. He's short-sighted, he's got a temper and he lies – sometimes.'

Jean glanced at Milo, and Dad told him that he had explained to me, as best he could, the strange beliefs some people held: that physical love between men and women was a sinful act, and a baby conceived in this way must therefore be somehow impure. But a clone created in a petri dish was untouched by that sin, and was in fact, an angel.

'So, Laura,' Jean placed an elegant, papery hand over mine. 'You understand?'

'That bit I understand.' I couldn't help wrinkling my nose. 'But what if the person was cloned from a murderer. Is the clone still an angel?'

'Aha!' Jean almost laughed. 'That is what the Society

believes, and that is why we know that what they preach is madness.'

Milo had finished his breakfast. He was fidgeting with a silver napkin-ring, eager for action. 'It beats me what they do all day,' he muttered.

Jean laughed out loud at that. 'The Society for Angels? They talk, they pray, they plot and they wait. But who knows what they would *do* with an angel?' He suddenly became serious. 'How they came to hear about Gwendal is a mystery to me. The doctor involved, and his assistant, are irreproachable. It is not in their interest to be careless of our secret.'

Milo leant forward, even more serious than Jean. 'Having met Nathan Culfire,' he said, 'I believe his evil is so tenacious, so watchful and devious, it can seep through bricks and mortar, tap into cables, into minds,' he tapped his head, then seeing my face, put an arm round my shoulder. 'I'm sorry, Lo, am I frightening you?'

'No,' I said.

When Raoul appeared, carrying a second pot of coffee, Milo decided it was time to ring Mum. His mobile would be useless in the mountains, Jean told him, so Dad wandered off to have a private conversation with mum in Raoul's kitchen, where the only phone was located.

I've never known a breakfast to last so long. After the coffee came croissants, for me, and brandy for Dad. And it wasn't even midday. We all wanted to start looking for Gwendal, but none of us could think how begin.

Apparently Gwendal had left directly after breakfast on Boxing Day. Jean thought he was in his room, until Raoul found him missing at lunchtime.

Gwendal had climbed down the icy steps from the fort to Saint-Luc. He had learnt that Gérard Bezain would be visiting his mother in Axat. He had climbed into Gérard's van and concealed himself under a pile of crates. When Gérard was making his visit to his mother, Gwendal must have leapt out and run into the town.

When Gérard returned to Saint-Luc and heard of Gwendal's disappearance, he searched his van and found a black leather mitten. Gwendal's. Gérard didn't know the truth about Gwendal. He thought him an orphan, a distant cousin of Jean's.

Where had he gone from Axat? Nobody knew. If he had thumbed a lift, no one had seen it. Enquiries had to be discreet for fear of alerting the police.

'Does it really matter?' I asked. 'Why can't the police know? They can find him better than we can. He might be in danger.'

'If the police find Gwendal, they will question him,' Jean said. 'It would be only a matter of time before his true identity was discovered. And then his life as an ordinary boy would be over.'

'Would you rather he was dead?' I cried.

'Laura,' Milo warned.

But Jean Tisseyre understood. 'Of course not, Laura.' He took my hand. 'And we will find him, very soon. If we don't then I shall do everything in my power to discover what has happened to him.' He fastened his dark eyes on me, and once again it bothered me. Not the look but something else. Something I couldn't quite grasp.

I withdrew my hand, trying to figure out what it was that I found so unsettling. Above me the sky in the dome had deepened to a brilliant blue. I wanted to breathe mountain air, to walk in the snow, above all to see the outside of this ancient fortress.

When I asked if I might walk in the snow, Jean recommended that we all go out together. So we put on our hats, our mountain boots and padded jackets and stepped out into the brilliant light. Snow lay in a soft, shadowed blanket over every mountain peak. The freezing air caught in my throat and stung my eyes. I felt light-headed and had to stop myself from giggling.

We descended a flight of steps, crossed the drive and stepped onto the plateau. I saw how the snowfield plunged into nowhere. Why had Gwendal been here on Christmas night? What had he run away from?

I expected Milo to start throwing snowballs, but he just stood there, gazing over the waves of mountains and giving no hint of what he was thinking.

I wheeled round, raising my arms. I think my intention was to fall back and make angels' wings in the snow, but instead I stopped in astonishment and gazed at the huge rock that loomed above us.

The fort was so different in daylight. The ancient stones were pale, almost silvery, and some of the window-panes were made of coloured glass; a fairytale fort instead of an ominous prison. At each end of the building stood a tower with a crenellated roof, a battlement in fact. But the towers only had three sides, the fourth being the cliff that rose behind them.

'What a hiding-place!' I said.

'Indeed,' said Jean, and he told us how he had restored the building to give himself a refuge – a secret place where he could escape and meditate. And then he spoke of his ancestors, the Cathars, who had hidden in the mountains to escape their enemies, the bloodthirsty crusaders. 'They considered themselves to be just and noble, Laura,' he said, 'those soldiers of the Pope. And yet they slaughtered and burned the Cathars, men, women and children, merely because their beliefs were different.'

'What did the Cathars believe?' I asked. 'Mum told me they were persecuted.'

Milo had walked to the edge of the plateau. He was gazing into the abyss when he heard my question and hurried back to us. I think he wanted to hear Jean's answer.

'They believed in the existence of the Prince of Darkness,' Jean raised his voice, 'that he ruled on earth and was responsible for all matter except our souls. Our souls alone belonged to God.'

'In other words the material world was of no importance,' Milo remarked with a smile.

Jean smiled back. 'Obviously I don't share my ancestors' beliefs,' he said. 'That is where they were burnt.' He pointed to a ring of stones close to the precipice. 'The crusaders dragged a rock-throwing machine up here. They breached the main wall and stormed into the building. Everyone inside was taken prisoner. A great pyre was built and one by one the Cathars were put to death. They went willingly into the flames, it is said. After all, their souls were safe. Their flesh was of no account.'

I felt the need to escape from their serious faces, so I leapt through the snow towards a line of rocks that ran from one of the towers to the edge of the plateau. When I had climbed the rocks I found myself looking down on the roofs of Saint-Luc. I could see the steps that wound down into the village and again I wondered, what was Gwendal running from? Perhaps he didn't run. Perhaps he intended to return.

I jumped from the rocks and ran back to Jean. 'Can I see Gwendal's room? He might have left a message.'

'There is no message, Laura,' Jean told me. 'We searched. We checked his computer – everything.'

'But still – I'd like to see.'

'Then come,' he held out his hand.

I took his hand and went with him, up the steps to the fort again. But Milo said he wanted a little more time under the sky. He would see the room later.

On the way to Gwendal's room Jean Tisseyre showed me the rest of his fort. He opened every door, revealed the view from every window. He was very proud of it. And if the ghosts of his ancestors roamed their old refuge they must have been contented ghosts, because I could only feel light and safety there.

At last I was led into a room that I recognized. I saw the stone walls, the banks of monitors, the four-poster bed and the big window with its view of the snowfield. And then I noticed that Isambard had gone.

'He took the robot,' I said.

'Of course. That is why I know he is safe. Isambard would let us know if it was not so. Can you think, Laura? Can you think where Gwendal would go?'

I shook my head. 'No. I've tried and tried but I can't think.'

Monsieur Tisseyre sat on the edge of the four-poster bed and looked through the window. We could see Milo on the snowfield. He was gazing up at the place where the pyre had been built, where the Cathars had jumped into the flames.

I began to study the flickering monitors. I moved books and papers. I looked under the pillows, under the bed. Then I tried the computer. Gwendal had made a great many programmes: fun programmes, stories, a diary. I began to read the account of his days at Fort Saint-Luc. Some of them were lonely days but not bad enough to run away from.

Jean sat and watched me. I would have thought a man like that would have something better to do. But perhaps other people were doing it for him.

The tone of Gwendal's diary was, if anything, more cheerful towards the end. He went climbing with Gérard's sons, even did some skiing, and he made friends on the internet. I skipped to the very end.

'The sun is shining today. Papa says my French has come on a lot. He has given me a card to my own bank account. It is a big account. Now, I can go anywhere.'

When I turned back to Jean Tisseyre he was leaning forward, his chin in his hand, like a statue – Rodin's *Thinker*.

'There's nothing here,' I said apologetically.

He just smiled. 'It's time for some food. We'll have another think when we have eaten. Food for the brain, eh? We will find him, Laura.'

'There's one thing I'd like to know,' I couldn't stop myself from asking.

'Yes?'

'You didn't mean this to happen, did you? You wanted Gwendal to live like a normal boy, with us, didn't you?'

'I did, yes. I had to face the truth. I am too old now, to be his father; life, for him, would be better spent with you. But I wanted to see him as much as I could, to be like a grandfather, perhaps.'

A startling thought occurred to me. 'You're Dr Zeigler, aren't you? The man who went to visit Gwendal at the clinic. You took him to the country, sometimes, and made friends with him.'

'You're very perceptive, Laura.'

'Was he surprised?'

'Surprised and pleased, I believe.'

'If he lives here, what will happen to him? You must be busy. Sometimes you're in Paris, I imagine. Or London, or New York. So what will Gwendal do, all alone?'

'It's not ideal,' he confessed. 'But he would be safe. The people of Saint-Luc are very special. They are fiercely loyal. They ask no questions, but if they know a friend is in trouble they will help, without hesitation. Gwendal has made friends already. In time he will go to school here.'

'And then what?'

'And then what?' Monsieur Tisseyre stood up. I think I was beginning to irritate him. I know I have a tendency to do that.

'Well, after school and that, what will happen?'

'Then he will be a man, Laura. And he can do as he wishes. It is only as a child that he needs protection. In ten years' time,' he gave one of his big shrugs, 'who knows what will happen. It is not long.'

I had nothing to say to that. Ten years had always

seemed far away to me. Suddenly it seemed closer. As I followed Jean out of the room I realized that I hadn't really wanted Gwendal to be happy here. I wanted him back with us. He'd become a part of our family, even if he was just another version of the famous and powerful man striding before me. I stared at his back, fascinated. Would Gwendal be like this? Exactly like this?

Raoul had laid a feast on the hall table. Soup and cold meat, masses of cheese and pâté, and crusty white bread.

Dad came bounding in, hungry from the cold, and probably from staring at ghostly pyres. We didn't mention the pyres or Cathar deaths again. In fact we didn't talk at all for a while. We just sloshed up the spicy soup and put our brains to rest. At least I did.

Until the bombshell came.

Clearing his throat, rather noisily I thought, Milo said he couldn't imagine what it must be like, seeing oneself as a child again, only from a different perspective.

Jean replied that children were lucky these days. Their childhood was recorded on film, on video . . . could actually be reproduced in virtual reality. He, himself, never had that advantage.

That wasn't what Dad had implied at all. 'But Jean,' he said 'you have living reality. You have Gwendal.'

Jean looked at us. He seemed disconcerted. And it was when I returned his gaze, and stared into those dark brown eyes, that it came to me, even before he told us.

'You have brown eyes,' I said. 'Gwendal's are blue.'

'His mother's were blue,' Jean said. 'He is exactly like her.'

'Wait a minute.' Milo began to look angry. 'What is

this . . . I thought . . . Has this all been a trick? All this fuss, this cloak-and-dagger stuff? If Mary is just a surrogate mother . . . Dammit, we really believed Gwendal was a . . . a clone.'

'He is,' Jean said quietly. 'A clone of my son.'

'What?' exclaimed Milo. 'Your *son*?'

I found I wasn't as surprised as Milo, but it was a shock all the same.

'I thought it wasn't an important detail,' Jean said.

'But I assumed it was your . . . Only you. No one mentioned . . .' Milo appeared to be at a loss. 'Jean, this is a shock. I can't . . .'

'I'm sorry. I was not scrupulous with the truth,' Jean said. 'I found it easier not to divulge his true identity, I can't explain why. I will have to tell you how it came about.'

'I think you will,' Milo said gravely.

So we listened, Dad and I, to one of the saddest stories I'd ever heard. I suppose there are lots of stories about people losing children, and they're all sad, but Jean Tisseyre had a gift, very different from his talent for making money. He could tell a story and make every little detail come alive, until you could almost feel it inside your mind. But perhaps this was the only story he ever told, or ever thought about.

He began at the point when the first Gwendal was four years old. Jean was already rich. He bought an old château in the country. His wife Véronique was enchanted with it. Over the next two years they restored it; they cleaned and painted, polished and planted, until it became a beautiful home, and a place where Jean could entertain and even do business.

Gwendal was not robust. He was short-sighted and slightly clumsy, but he was already proving to have a talent for figures. He was also a kind and generous child, and very gentle with insects and animals. The lake became his obsession. He caught tiny fish, tadpoles, newts, dragonflies and beetles; he would examine them carefully in their glass jars and then return them to the water.

When Gwendal was six Véronique became pregnant again. All three of them were very excited.

One icy midwinter day, when Jean was in Paris, Gwendal told his mother he could hear the frogs calling. She said it was too early, and he must on no account go near the lake without her.

He nodded solemnly and went away. Véronique's baby was due. She felt tired and heavy. She fell asleep in an armchair by the kitchen range. Gwendal put on his boots, his coat and his scarf. He took an empty glass jar from the pantry and walked down to the lake.

The housekeeper, Adèle, saw him from an upstairs window. She called out to him, and then hurried down to Véronique. The two women ran outside together, calling his name. He was kneeling at the far end of the jetty, with one arm deep in the water. '*Mes lunettes*!' he shouted. His spectacles had slipped off his nose and fallen in the lake.

With horror the two women watched him lose his balance and topple into the water. He didn't re-emerge. And before Adèle could stop her, Véronique was on the jetty, peering into the lake and then plunging after him. 'I can't see him. I can't find him, Adèle!' She was sobbing as she came to the surface.

'Poor Adèle,' said Jean. 'What could she do? She tried

to reach Véronique, but my wife was heavy with the baby, and struggling to find her little drowned boy.'

Milo and I didn't dare to say a word.

'Adèle's husband, Gilles, was in the workshop,' Jean continued. 'He was our gardener. He heard the crying and ran to the lake. It was too late, of course. Véronique was alive when they brought her to the bank, but by the time the doctor came, she had gone, and so had the baby. It was a little girl.

'Gwendal had not been found when I got home. But the news had reached the village. Many people came to help us, among them was a boy, a teenager who had lost his whole family. He found Gwendal. "He is so cold, so cold," the boy kept saying. "He is ice." And he was crying. It's strange but for a day my eyes were dry. It was too much to comprehend.' There were tears in his eyes now, and I knew that Jean Tisseyre was not the man in the story of *The Little Prince*, the businessman who had never smelled a flower, or loved anyone. It was not an heir he wanted, it was his own little boy.

'That's terrible Jean, so terrible,' Milo said quietly.

'What happened to the teenager?' I asked, trying to shift the subject a little. I didn't want us all to cry.

'He stayed with me,' Jean said. 'He stayed forever. He is Raoul.'

Perhaps we should have guessed.

'That is why he cannot accept Gwendal,' Jean said. 'He held a frozen boy in his arms, and now he is alive again. He feels it should not be.'

'Is Gwendal like him then?' I asked.

'Oh, yes.' Jean told us it was something Raoul said, all

those years ago, that had brought us here today. 'He is ice,' Raoul said, and it put into Jean's mind, the image of a frozen boy, frozen in time. And so that is what he had done. He had his son frozen – just in case there came a time when someone could make him live again. Cloning hadn't entered his mind. And then he heard that experiments were being conducted; a mouse had been cloned, a sheep. Jean had access to an infinite fortune. He began the search for a team who could help him. And he found it.

'You know the rest,' he looked at Milo. 'When the time was right my – envoys if you like, began another search – to find the perfect family. Perfect but desperate enough to risk breaking the law. They found five. But it was not easy.'

'Five?' I could feel my eyes popping.

'Three in France, one in England, another in Scotland.'

'So there are five Gwendals?' It was difficult to imagine, and I could see that Milo was finding it as hard as I was.

Jean shook his head. 'Two . . . experiments did not succeed. One died at birth, the fourth survived for a month. You see how special Gwendal is.'

'Why did you give him the same name as . . . the other one?' I asked.

'I didn't. Mary chose it from a list I made. Most of the names were English. I wasn't going to include Gwendal but something made me, and out of twenty names she chose that one.' Jean shook his head, still puzzled and yet glad.

All at once Dad swung out of his chair and began

pacing up and down. 'He would have been special anyway,' he muttered. 'Jean, we've got to find him before they do, the Society for Angels.'

I knew where Gwendal had gone. He had always wanted to find out who he was, always wanted to meet the man he believed himself to be.

'Gwendal thought he was, well, you,' I said to Jean. 'Did you tell him about the other Gwendal?'

'I did,' said Jean. 'I think he was a little bit shocked. I told him on Christmas Day. That night I found him wandering outside. I should have been afraid for him then, but he said he was just enjoying the snow. I thought he would get over it.'

'I know where he is!' I said.

'You do?'

'Laura?'

Their faces wore almost the same expression. They had both been a father to Gwendal.

'He's gone to the place where the other Gwendal drowned,' I said. 'He hasn't run away.' It was too much to explain how I knew this. I hated the picture that had suddenly fixed itself in my mind: Gwendal standing beside the lake where his first self hadn't managed to go on living. On a cold, midwinter day.

5
Visiting the past

What happened next was inevitable. Milo wanted to drive to the château.

'Three days have passed,' said Jean. 'Adèle's daughter, Mathilde, would have contacted me. She lives there now, with her husband and son.

'She might not have seen him,' I put in. 'He's shy. He wouldn't have rung the bell.'

'I want to go there, Jean,' insisted Milo. 'It's a starting point, and I feel useless here.'

It disturbed Jean Tisseyre, this determination of Milo's to visit a place where ghosts might lie in wait.

'I have never been back,' he confessed. 'I have allowed Adèle and her family to live there for the rest of their lives, if they want. They keep it just as it was. Raoul goes from time to time, but I . . .' he studied his hands, flexing the fingers.

He agreed to give Milo a map and directions, but pointed out that it would take almost a day to reach the place. He showed us a photograph: the château stood at the end of a long avenue. It had been built in the sixteenth century, Jean said. I gazed at a near-perfect building, four storeys high, with long blue-shuttered windows and a tall grey roof. Two thick chimneys poked out of the top and beneath them, like a row of portholes, small round windows had been set into the slates. Which room belonged to the first Gwendal, I wondered? And where was the lake?

Adèle was in her eighties now, Jean told us. Her husband had died but her daughter, Mathilde and her family lived there with her. Mathilde's two sons were married; one of them lived at the château with his wife, Sophie.

'So you see, it's not a sad place.' Jean could not quite manage a smile. 'I make sure that the family are comfortable. In other words I pay the bills. The château is theirs – all but two rooms. They are always ready for my visit, but . . .' he shrugged. 'One day I will go.'

In spite of the happy family filling his house, it sounded a bit like a shrine to me.

Milo looked at the photograph, for several seconds before saying, 'We have to give it a chance, even if Gwendal hasn't been seen there.'

Jean agreed, but without much enthusiasm. Raoul would prepare everything for our journey, he said. And he would telephone Mathilde, to warn her of our arrival. But we must not state the true reason for our visit. They must think that Gwendal was Milo's son, who had gone missing on a family holiday.

I didn't sleep so soundly on my second night in Fort Saint-Luc. I had so much on my mind. I was certain that Gwendal would go to the château. Before he left us he had already embarked on the quest to find out who he really was. The shock, even the excitement of hearing the truth, would have obliterated everything else on his mind, and driven him to Château Mirande.

It was very late when I heard Milo's footsteps in the passage outside my room. I didn't call out to him. I'm sure he assumed I was asleep. I lay for another hour, feeling more wide awake than ever. But when I went to the window I saw that someone else was awake; lights from the fort blazed across the snow.

I left my room and crept to the end of the passage. I don't know if I meant to speak to Jean Tisseyre, but I found myself on the cold steps that led down to the hall. I reached the first spiral when the treads suddenly narrowed and curved steeply, and then I stopped. Voices drifted up to me. Harsh, distraught voices. Jean and Raoul were arguing. I couldn't understand the words, but it sounded as though Raoul were pleading with Jean. What had so distressed him? Could it be our intended visit to Château Mirande?

Mystified, I turned and tiptoed back up the stairs. What did the château mean to Raoul, I wondered? Remembering that he had found the drowned boy there, I imagined he would think it a gloomy place. Raoul had been against Jean's macabre experiment from the beginning. But I must not think of it as macabre. The experiment produced Gwendal.

I wandered on, past my own door and past Milo's. I was making for Gwendal's room, though I had been only half aware of this. The narrow passages were lit by jewel-like bulbs, half-concealed in the rough stone. I walked in my own shadow, as though it belonged to a stranger. It loomed and swung now behind and now before me, and

I began to feel the ghosts. Imaginary Cathars, creeping beside me, terrified by the thunder of rocks pounding their walls, the roaring of the Pope's soldiers and the stench of their dreadful fires.

When I came to Gwendal's room I almost fell into it. Reaching for a switch I flooded the room with light, and the ghosts receded. The rows of flickering monitors rushed me back into the present and my heart stopped thumping.

Most of the screens showed a different view of the fort: the passages, the hall, Raoul's kitchen and the deep steps leading up from the town. Andy's rats came as a surprise. There they were, snuggled together in their cage on Andy's floor. So Mum had rescued lonely Isidore, and put him there to enjoy the company of Drift and Snow. Or perhaps she had thought to remind Gwendal of his other home.

An unexpected rush of homesickness swept over me. I could do with Andy right now, I thought. Dad had seemed far away, all day, wrapped in his own thoughts.

I watched the rats for a moment and then glanced at the last screen. Isambard, said the sticker above it. Previously this screen had been blank, but now it showed black water touched by moonlight, so that it shimmered with stars. At any other time I would have found it beautiful. Now, thinking of the lake at Château Mirande, I was terrified.

I gazed at the glittering water for maybe a minute, waiting to see a face, a figure, anything to tell me where it was, but the screen went blank again. For an hour I watched, or maybe longer. I sat on the big four-poster, dozed off, woke again and waited, staring at the blank screen until my eyes ached. At last I fell asleep.

It was still dark when I woke up. I had crawled under the covers on Gwendal's bed. I could hear my name being called and dragging myself out of sleep, I ran to the door, opening it just as Milo was about to step inside.

'Lo, thank goodness. Have you been sleeping in there?'

I told him about Isambard's screen, the starry black water.

'It could mean anything,' he said. How could we guess? He was already dressed. Breakfast was waiting and food for the journey packed in his rucksack.

Raoul was not the smiling cook today. He served our big English breakfast in silence. Sipping his strong black coffee, Jean waited until Raoul left the room and then he said to me, 'Raoul is upset. You have noticed, yes? He does not like the place – Château Mirande. He does not think you should go there, Laura.'

'Me? Why?'

'It is not a good place for children,' he says. 'He thinks you should stay here while your father goes alone.'

I looked at Milo.

'Perhaps Raoul is right,' he said.

'Look!' I plonked down my knife. 'I'm not a child for one thing. And it was my idea, right?'

'Right,' said Milo with a crooked smile.

Jean regarded me thoughtfully. '*Bien sûr*, Laura,' he said.

The sky was beginning to fill with blue light when we left the fort. We descended the icy steps backwards, and when we reached the road, I turned to see the little town at sunrise. It lay calmly cradled in the mountains, its wavy tiled roofs slowly turning pink; a place where fairy-tales began.

Gérard had been phoned and the Trekker was in the street outside his house. The oil had been checked and the tank filled; it was ready for its next mission.

'Take care,' Gérard said as we climbed inside. 'If there is trouble, you must telephone.' He thrust a scrap of paper at Milo. 'This number you must call, if you cannot reach Monsieur Tisseyre.' He slammed the car door and stood back. As Milo started the engine he moved away. When I looked back, he was still watching us, but he didn't wave. His hands were in his pockets and he was frowning.

'They all look so grim today. You'd think we were going to a funeral,' I said thoughtlessly.

Milo didn't reply. He was concentrating on the road ahead. In the early light we could see the dangers that had been hidden by the dark. Turning a corner we would get a sudden view of awesome cliffs and rocky precipices. We passed several little towns, none of them quite as pretty as Saint-Luc, though the houses were very similar with their rounded tiles and white walls.

I began to dream a bit, and another hour had passed before I realized that the ice and snow had vanished; the mountains were behind us and we were plunging down into wine country. Vineyards stretched for miles around us, cropped and winter-brown. And the blue sky of the mountains was replaced by a blanket of dull grey. It began to drizzle.

'Hm,' Milo muttered. 'I don't feel like a tourist any more.'

'I never did.' I said.

We stopped for our snack on the edge of a romantic-looking avenue, and Milo consulted the map. Jean's familiar red ink ran north in a steady line, and then looped to the left. I stared at the place where it stopped, and wondered why everyone was so afraid of Château Mirande. The tragedy there took place so long ago, surely the place had recovered. Time heals everything, they say. Adèle had managed to go on living there.

'Will we see Adèle?' I asked Milo.

'Probably not. She's over eighty and wanders, apparently.' He touched his head. 'She lives in the past.'

'I hope it wasn't all bad then,' I murmured.

'Don't be morbid,' Milo said.

I wasn't being morbid. I wanted to hear her version of events, so that I could remember every detail. When Gwendal came back he would want to talk about it. He would want to know the good things as well as the bad.

The sun appeared, very briefly, with our first view of the château. An avenue of tall, naked trees took us towards ornate wrought-iron gates; behind them we saw the house. It was just as it had looked in the photograph and yet, because of what I knew, I felt it to be dense with memories. Terrible things had happened here, and reached far into the world.

We stopped outside the gates and Milo said, 'Can you get the bell, Lo? *Lo*?' He had to raise his voice to get through to me. I was still locked in my thoughts.

There was a bell-pull on the stone gatepost, and a

small brass panel with an intercom. I jumped down and pulled on the bell while Milo waited in the car.

' 'Ello,' said a voice in my ear.

'McCool,' I said. 'Milo and Laura.'

'*Entrez*, Mademoiselle!'

The gates opened and I followed the car into the round driveway. Obligingly, the gates closed behind me.

Mathilde was already on the step. She was the rosiest person I've ever seen. Everything about her was plump and curved. She was only a head taller than me and her smile wrapped right into her round cheeks. Her hair was grey and bubbly.

Before Milo could introduce himself, Mathilde grabbed me in a big hug. Anyone would have thought I was her long lost child. I stepped back, rather breathlessly and said, 'I'm Laura,' in case she'd made a mistake.

She hadn't. 'Welcome! Welcome!' She ushered us through a tiled hall and into a large bright room. The place seemed to be full of cushions. There were two sofas and four armchairs, and everyone one of them held seven or eight plump squares. They might just as well have been beds.

'*Ma mère* makes these,' said Mathilde, indicating the pillowy cushions we were trying to tuck ourselves into.

'Inside is the goose feather,' she explained, 'and outside – she make.'

We dutifully examined the covers. There were panels of tapestry, crocheted squares and knitted patches. Some had been embroidered with strange little figures and others made into animal shapes: a pig, a cat, a dog and two ducks.

'All day she do this,' Mathilde looked almost apologetic.

I wanted to ask if we would be meeting Adèle, but didn't feel I could put it in quite the right way, just yet.

Mathilde wasn't too sure why we had come. Monsieur Tisseyre had mentioned a child, my brother. No name had been given. She would fetch her daughter-in-law, Sophie. The men were still at work, Mathilde explained, but Sophie spoke good English.

Milo threw a warning glance at me. Mathilde's family obviously knew nothing about the second Gwendal, not even his name. It was going to be difficult to explain why we thought my brother had come here.

While we waited for Sophie I went to the long window that overlooked the garden. A stone wall enclosed the paved terrace that ran the length of the building, and two stone lions sat either side of a flight of steps leading to the lawn. At the end of the long lawn a row of leafless trees could not hide the glimmer of water: the lake.

'I can see the lake,' I whispered.

As Dad got up to join me, Sophie came in. She was as different from Mathilde as it was possible to be. Her face was sharp, her lips thin, her short hair pale and very straight.

'It's a beautiful place, isn't it?' she said, perching on the edge of a chair.

Milo agreed with her.

'We are lucky to live here, you think?' It sounded like a challenge.

'Indeed,' said Milo. 'But I can see that you look after

it, everything is very . . . nice. The garden . . .' He waved a hand towards a garden he hadn't seen. 'It's all beautiful,' he finished lamely.

She came straight to the point. 'And you think your son came here?'

'Er . . . yes, we do.' He glanced at me. 'It's just an idea.'

'Why, monsieur?'

'I . . .' Milo hadn't planned ahead. For once, he couldn't think of a story.

Mathilde came to the rescue. Bustling in with a tray, she began to arrange cups and saucers on a low table.

'He's very morbid,' I said quickly. As I spoke I began to construct a life for Gwendal; a story that would explain our presence. 'He likes to visit scenes of crime, that sort of thing.'

Milo bent his head over his cup, but I could see the smile of approval on his face.

Sophie frowned. 'There has been no crime here.'

'But a tragedy, Madame,' said Milo. 'A terrible tragedy.' As he looked at an imagined glimmer of water through the window, I saw his eyes begin to lose their cautious woody colour. In a few seconds they were bright green.

'That was a long time ago.' Sophie exchanged glances with her mother. 'It is forgotten.'

'Not by Monsieur Tisseyre,' Milo reminded them. 'It altered his life. Gwendal . . .' The name was out. It was too late to take it back. 'Gwendal, my son, is Monsieur Tisseyre's godson.'

'Your son also is Gwendal,' Mathilde looked shocked, but I noticed that Sophie didn't show the slightest surprise.

'Yes, my son was named Gwendal in memory, as it were.' Milo's green eyes began to wander as he spoke. 'He was staying with Monsieur Tisseyre. He often does. They're fond of each other. Naturally Gwendal was very affected when he heard the story; Véronique and her son, both drowning. He wanted to see the place for himself. Monsieur Tisseyre wouldn't bring him here, so Gwendal came on his own – we believe.'

Sophie's eyes narrowed. 'But to come so far alone. How old is he?'

'He's nine,' Milo said. 'But very resourceful.'

'Yes?' Sophie looked sceptical.

'Are you sure you haven't seen a boy in the grounds?' Milo asked hopefully. 'Near the house, perhaps. Nothing?'

'*Non*,' said Mathilde.

'Nothing,' added Sophie.

A cold, wary feeling swept through me. It happens when you know someone is not being entirely truthful. 'Could we see Adèle?' I asked.

The women stared at me and Sophie said, 'She's not well. She has been seeing . . . ghosts.'

For a moment we were stumped and then I had another idea. 'Can I see where the other Gwendal used to sleep?' I asked. 'His room? Is it the same as . . . as when he left it?'

It was a lucky guess. The room was kept just as it was, Sophie told us. On Monsieur Tisseyre's orders they had changed nothing. Sometimes, Adèle dusted the toys, let in fresh air, but that was all. And, yes, it would be perfectly all right for me to see the room.

Mathilde took me up a grand staircase to the second

floor, where I followed her down a long carpeted passage. We stopped at a door right at the end, but when Mathilde opened it she gave an exclamation of surprise. The curtains had been drawn back, she explained; usually they were closed to prevent the sun from bleaching the furniture.

There was no sun today.

I felt uncomfortable standing in a nursery crammed with the past, and yet empty of the boy who used to play there. There was a quilt embroidered with ducks, on the small blue bed, and the walls were covered with pictures of farmyard animals. A teddy-bear was propped against the headboard and on the floor, beside the bed, toys sat in a neat row. The last things a little boy had touched. There was a clockwork polar bear, a big dog on wheels, a red wooden engine with a string of open carriages behind it, and a tiny ancient car.

I reached for a row of books on a shelf behind the bed, and then stopped. Should I touch them?

'Yes, yes,' said Mathilde. 'You look. I come back soon.' She went off, with an anxious frown. Perhaps she was looking for someone?

The room wasn't spooky exactly, it was just sad. I wondered how Gwendal would have felt, looking at the toys that had belonged to his other self. I tried to see it from his point of view, but it was beyond me.

The books were all in French, of course. I leafed through them, one by one, and then I came to *Le Petit Prince*. It gave me a jolt to see it there, even though it's probably the equivalent of *Winnie-the-Pooh* for French children.

I carried the book to the light, passing a big cupboard that stood sideways on to the window. Something caught my eye; something half-hidden between the cupboard and the window. It was an old woman, grey and small with a tiny wizened face. I stifled a scream as she smiled. I realized it must be Adèle.

She put a finger to her lips. 'Sssh!' Her big pale eyes fastened themselves on the book. '*Le Petit Prince*!' she said.

'*Oui*!' I replied. '*Je suis Laura.*'

So far so good. I hoped she wouldn't expect too much of me. But then she began to whisper in French, on and on, scarcely taking a breath between sentences.

'I'm sorry,' I stuck a finger into my chest. '*Anglaise, moi.*'

'Huh?' Adèle stared at me while I wished I'd paid more attention in French lessons.

'*Je cherche un garçon,*' I said at last. Was it the wrong thing to have said?

'*Un garçon?*' she whispered. 'Gwendal?'

What could I have said? I didn't want to confuse her. 'Gwendal, *mon frère.*' I spoke very softly because she seemed not to want anyone to hear us.

'Ah!' She pointed at the window pane. '*Hier, Gwendal était là,*' she said.

I followed the line of her finger and saw the wide stretch of water. The surrounding reeds with their pale winter stalks emphasized the darkness of the lake.

'Gwendal,' she said again.

I noticed that they hadn't even removed the fatal jetty. It reached over the water on thin wooden supports and I could almost see the small figure dangerously balanced at the far end.

'Yes, Gwendal,' I repeated.

She clutched my arm so tightly it hurt.

There was an exclamation from the doorway. '*Maman*!' said Mathilde. '*Non, Maman.*'

'I'm sorry,' I murmured, 'I didn't meant to upset her.'

Gently Mathilde tried to prise her mother's fingers away from my arm. She spoke quietly, in French, and gradually the old woman relaxed her grip.

'She was talking about Gwendal,' I told Mathilde.

'Memories. All long ago.' Mathilde led her mother away.

There were tears in Adèle's eyes when she looked back at me. Somehow, I didn't think she was speaking of 'long ago'.

I ran downstairs and found Milo talking to Sophie in the hall. He was about to make a quick search of the grounds, and I was glad he hadn't left me alone with the three women.

'What are we looking for?' I asked as Sophie let us out through the french windows.

'Anything,' Milo said. 'Any sign that Gwendal might have been here.'

Sophie closed the windows behind us and we descended the stone steps down to the lawn.

Milo headed for the lake. 'Sophie didn't seem very keen on this,' he said grimly. 'Why do I have an uncomfortable feeling that she's hiding something?'

I told him about my meeting with Adèle. 'She didn't really frighten me,' I said. 'She talked about Gwendal over and over, but it was only natural; after all I was in his room, looking for a boy.' Milo tucked my hand in his.

'She was upset,' I went on. 'Just before Mathilde took her away she said something I couldn't understand. I knew the word but I was so frightened I suddenly couldn't remember. It was *hier*.'

'*Hier*?' Milo stopped and looked at me. 'It means yesterday.'

'Yesterday?' I said faintly. '"*Hier, Gwendal était là*!" And she pointed at the lake. Dad, d'you think she really saw him, saw *our* Gwendal?'

'I think it's very possible.'

'And d'you think she told *them*? Mathilde and Sophie?'

'If she did, then they dismissed it as her rambling.' He began to press on, and then stopped again. 'Unless they're lying.'

'Not Mathilde,' I said.

'No, not Mathilde. But I wouldn't put anything past Sophie. What's more, she seems to be in charge of that household.'

We walked on to the lake. It was a grim place, desolate and dark. The impenetrable water was utterly still. Not a bird, not a ripple broke the awful deadness. As we walked past the reeds we noticed, here and there, a snapped stalk, and several lay flat on the pebbles. We came to the jetty. It rocked violently when Milo stood on it. He only took a few steps, however, before he stopped and picked up a board. It had been broken in two, very recently. The jagged edge was white against the old wood.

'I was told that no one comes here,' Milo said. 'But someone has, and very recently.' He jumped off the jetty. 'Gwendal!' he called. 'Gwendal!'

A duck clattered out of the reeds on the far bank, croaking anxiously.

'Dad, it'll scare them,' I said, 'especially Adèle.'

'Hm!' He stared across the lake to the woods in the distance. 'There'll be a wall or a fence beyond those trees, but nothing too big for a determined boy to climb. Let's go, Laura. We've seen enough and they,' he nodded at the château, 'aren't going to give anything away.'

Mathilde was upset to hear we wouldn't stop for a meal. The men would be home soon, she said. They would like to meet us.

'It's getting dark,' Milo told her. 'We should be on our way. We'll stop at a bar in an hour or two.'

Sophie showed us to the door, while Mathilde followed, muttering about the long journey ahead, and that the child should eat.

Milo turned and thanked them both for their trouble.

'No trouble, Monsieur.' It was Sophie who spoke. 'We are caretakers only. I'm sorry your time was wasted.'

'Not wasted,' Milo muttered. 'Not at all,' and we climbed into the Trekker.

The wrought-iron gates slid open, then closed behind us. I looked back and waved, but the door of Château Mirande had already been shut.

A mist was rising from the fields, and as we drove down the avenue I noticed a grey car, parked off the road. Its bonnet was just visible between two trees, almost as if it were hiding.

When I glanced through the rear window, I saw that

the car had emerged onto the road. It began to follow us. As it moved closer the headlights came on, and suddenly I was afraid.

6
Phantoms in the snow

'Dad, there's a car following us.' I clutched his arm.

Milo looked in the driving mirror. 'It's probably just going our way,' he said.

'No. It was hiding in the trees. It came out when we passed.'

Milo shrugged. 'We'll see.'

We travelled on for several miles. It was a quiet, rural area and there were very few cars on the road. Whenever I looked back the grey car was behind us, sometimes quite distant and then drawing closer. It was getting dark, but I had memorized the shape and position of the headlights. They were square and boxy-looking with little hoods.

When we came to a village, Milo pulled in to the kerb. The grey car drove past and disappeared.

'There,' said Milo. 'Gone. It was just a coincidence. Let's eat, shall we?'

I didn't feel any easier. But I was desperately hungry.

We found a café that looked bright and popular. In fact the whole village seemed to have congregated there for a chat. We had bowls of hot cassoulet and ate a whole loaf between us before we felt ready to tackle the long journey ahead.

By the time we left the café night and fallen. In half an hour, the grey sky had become inky black.

I fell asleep long before we reached the mountains. The car, jerking to a halt woke me up again. Milo was staring into the driving mirror, while the engine ticked slowly.

'Don't be alarmed,' he said softly. 'Could you have a look at those headlights behind us? Do you recognize them?'

I turned and looked. A car had stopped about fifty metres behind us. Even at that distance I recognized the headlights. 'It's the same car, Dad.'

'Then you're right, Lo. We're being followed.' Milo drummed his fingers on the steering wheel. 'We'll have to phone Jean. The mobile's useless here. We'll stop at a petrol station.' He drove off, very fast, and I watched the stranger's headlights move after us.

We found a petrol station and parked under the lights, in full view of the attendant's window, just in case. I squeezed into the phone booth with Dad. I didn't want to be alone out there. While Milo spoke to Jean I watched the forecourt for a sign of the grey car, but it didn't appear.

Milo replaced the receiver. 'Jean wants us to keep going,' he said. 'The problem will be dealt with, whatever that means. He's a mysterious man, Jean Tisseyre.'

We filled up with petrol and swung on to the road again. Several cars passed us, going in the opposite direction, but although I craned my neck for ages, watching the road behind, the sinister hooded lights seemed to have vanished.

I couldn't sleep again. All my senses were on alert. I made Dad sing with me, and then we played games: quizzes and 'I-think-I-spy' and charades without actions.

It began to snow. Just a few drifting flakes at first, but soon the night was white with dancing snow. It whirled into our headlights, hitting the windscreen like flying stars. Not so good for Milo. We were in the mountains now and had to move painfully slowly through the storm. Every time we turned a bend I thought our wheels would lock and we'd spin off the road.

Things couldn't get worse, you might have thought, but they did. I saw Milo glance into the driving mirror and swear. When I looked behind us, the hooded head-lights were there again.

'Who are they? What do they want?' Fear squeezed my throat and my voice came out in a thin trickle. 'Oh, Dad, who are they?' We were trapped between a snowstorm and someone who was not a friend.

Milo squeezed my hand. 'Lo, it's going to be all right. Before we reach Saint-Luc there'll be a forest, remember. We can get up speed there, maybe hide while they go past.' He took a deep breath and said firmly, 'Lo, we'll make it.'

I didn't see how we could escape whoever it was. Culfire most probably, I thought. Nathan Culfire with several henchmen, even worse than the grey skaters.

'It's a wolf,' I muttered. 'That's what it is, out for another bite of Milo.'

Dad laughed and I felt my spirits lift a little.

'I've seen off bigger wolves than this,' he said. 'So if it's a wolf, it had better look out for Milo McCool.'

I managed to smile but when I looked back yet again, I saw that the other car was getting closer.

Then something extraordinary happened. Out of the flying snow a form materialized: a tall, hooded figure. It appeared on our left and then it was gone. Yet I sensed it was still beside us, hidden in the snow.

Milo stared ahead, saying nothing.

'Did you see it, Dad?' I whispered.

'Yes.'

As he spoke another figure drifted into view, this time on our right. It made no attempt to stop us, but like the other, it seemed to stay close, gliding through the white storm like a ghost, and my terror was replaced by a strange calm. I felt as though I were being carried in a dream, and as long as I remained there, as long as I didn't wake, I would be safe.

I was jolted back to reality as we turned a slow and dangerous corner, and then came to a halt. A row of lights were strung across the road, their beams thrown into our faces, momentarily blinding.

'What the . . .?' Milo shielded his eyes with one hand.

Perhaps after all we hadn't escaped. I squeezed my eyes tight shut and buried my face in Dad's sleeve. Waiting.

'Lo, it's all right,' Dad said softly.

When I looked up, the torchlights ahead had been turned away from us. Their beams lit the sparkling, snowy air, while the men who held them were frozen in our own headlights. There were about six of them. They wore hooded macs, waterproofs and big sturdy boots. Some of them smiled solemnly. They were not ghosts. One lifted his hand as though in greeting. It was Gérard.

The line of men parted, ushering us through. As we passed them, Milo lowered his window. 'Gérard?' he said.

A man stepped forward, his head and shoulders white with snow. '*Vous êtes en mains sûres*, Monsieur McCool,' he said. 'Continue. You are safe.' His voice was low and comforting.

'*Merci*,' Dad said gravely.

We slid away from them and when I looked back they had closed ranks again. I watched the shadowy line recede in clouds of whirling ice, and I wondered what would happen when the next car turned that treacherous corner. I knew that Gérard would not let it through. As I turned back, with a shudder, I thought I heard a distant rumble, but decided it was only in my head. I sensed a violence out there, in the mysterious white night.

We came to the forest and at last a clear view of the road ahead. A few drifting flakes spun through the canopy above us but they hadn't yet settled. Milo put his foot down and we sped through the tunnel of dark trees.

The houses of Saint-Luc looked like buildings in a fairytale, all icy white and sparkling in the streetlights. I was surprised to see so many people about, stamping through the snow, carrying wood and baskets, calling to each other, closing shutters, sweeping paths. Delicious smells of baking came from briefly opened doors. It felt so safe.

As we turned into the shelter beside Gérard's house a stocky figure come out of the door. By the time we had climbed out of the Trekker he was in the road, waiting for us.

'Monsieur McCool!' The voice was familiar.

'Raoul?' asked Milo.

We could scarcely see his face for the hat that was pulled down over his eyebrows, and the padded collar that reached over his chin.

'*Oui*! It is Raoul.' He grabbed my hand. 'Come. I help you climb.'

Once again we mounted the icy steps up to the fort. But now flying snow made our first attempt seem almost easy. This time our progress was much slower, but the wind had dropped and at least I could feel my fingers. Every few steps Raoul would reach down and haul me upwards. It seemed to cost him no effort at all, and I was very aware of his tremendous strength.

Jean Tisseyre was waiting for us. He stood under his lantern, gazing at the snow, and I ran out of it and bowled right into the expensive suit and hugged him. He patted my head and hugged me back.

'Quite a day you've had, *chérie*,' he said.

He took us into the hall where we flung off our thick clothes and warmed our hands by the blazing fire. Jean knew about Gérard, of course, because after Dad's call he had sought his help. But Jean couldn't tell us what would happen, out there on the treacherous road.

'Will we ever know if it was Nathan Culfire in the car?' I asked.

Jean shrugged. 'Maybe.'

I had a vision of the car plunging into a chasm while a row of hooded men followed its fall with their torchlight. Could it be construed as murder, I wondered?

Milo told Jean everything that had happened at Château Mirande, but when he mentioned my strange meeting with Adèle, Jean rubbed his forehead and said, 'I haven't seen her for a long time. I am ashamed.'

'I'm sure Gwendal has been there,' said Milo. 'Though Sophie wouldn't have it. She believes Adèle is lost in her memories.'

Jean looked thoughtful. 'You know I think that Sophie resents living there,' he said.

'She doesn't have to,' I pointed out.

'No she doesn't,' Jean agreed. 'But she is the sort who takes advantage. Do you understand, *chérie*?'

I liked being called *chérie*.

They began to discuss Gwendal's next destination, and why we were followed. Had Sophie seen Gwendal after all, and betrayed him? Had she been approached by Culfire? Perhaps it was a case of blackmail, or ransom?

My spinning thoughts gave me a headache, so I just let Milo and Jean drone on, this way and that, while Raoul poured wine, and English tea for me. I was on the point of nodding off when Jean said, 'I must show you something in Gwendal's room. I don't know what to make of it.'

Immediately I was wide awake. As we followed Jean down the shadowy passages my brain came to life again.

Once again we faced the battery of little screens on Gwendal's wall. It was the last one that troubled Jean: Isambard's screen. At the moment it was blank.

'But look,' said Jean. 'I'll play the recording. Everything is taped. This came through at eight o'clock tonight.' He pressed a key and the screen began to flicker. A street appeared. An English street because there was a bus stop in the foreground, clearly marked. The camera (or rather

Isambard) moved slowly. Occasionally it stopped and looked over a fence into a window.

'Wait a minute,' Milo exclaimed. 'That's our street.'

It was. As the camera moved on, closer and closer, I knew where it was going to stop. It did. I found myself looking at our own gate, and beyond it the front door. All the lights in the house were out. The car had gone.

'Where's Mary?' Milo murmured.

And then it dawned on me. 'Dad, it's New Year's Eve!'

'Good grief. I'd forgotten.'

I began to think about the person outside our house. If it was Gwendal, what would he do now? And if it wasn't, then someone had stolen Isambard.

I'm sure this thought had occurred to Milo. 'We must go home,' he said.

'It would seem the right thing,' Jean agreed.

Raoul hadn't forgotten New Year's Eve. When we got back to the hall there was a large iced cake on the table, and a bottle of champagne. The very best, I imagine.

'*Dix minutes!*' Raoul declared, holding the bottle aloft.

I was allowed one glass. And then Dad had practically to carry me to bed. I fell asleep immediately. An hour later I was wide awake again. The luminous dial on my watch told me it was 2.00 a.m. I couldn't think what had woken me. A nightmare that I couldn't remember? As I lay there, wondering, the details of our extraordinary day began to swim through my mind. But it was the men on the mountain road who stole out of my head and invaded the room; grey and faceless they drifted through curtains of snow that fell from above me and covered my bed.

A sudden thought made me sit up, gasping. Who were

the men walking beside us? The men without torches? Were they part of Gérard's group – or something else?

I slid under the covers and stared into the darkness, while the hooded figures moved in and out of my thoughts. Eventually, they sent me to sleep.

I was the first to wake, except for Raoul. When I walked into the hall he was laying the table for breakfast.

'*Bonjour*, Laura! You are hungry?' he said.

'Today, I'm very hungry,' I replied. 'Do you think it's the mountain air?'

He stared at me for a moment, not quite comprehending, and then he said, 'Mountain air?' as though he were testing the words.

I nodded and sat down, while he fussed around the table; his eyes, under very thick eyebrows, kept darting in my direction, and I found myself wondering how so much hair had managed to grow on his brow, and so very little on his head. It was as if all his hair had slipped down until it met the bridge of his rather impressive nose.

After about five minutes of this darting-look game, Raoul suddenly said, 'It is not a good place, Château Mirande.'

'But beautiful,' I said.

'But beautiful,' he conceded.

I wanted him to tell me more about the château but realized this wouldn't be easy, his English being limited and ditto my French. Anyway, we were saved the bother of trying because Jean came in with his newspaper. Pulling a chair close to mine, he asked me how I'd slept after such an eventful day.

I told him the truth. That some of the events had been

too strange to shake off. 'What happened to the grey car?' I asked him. 'Do you know?'

'It never appeared,' he said. 'Gérard contacted me early this morning.'

'But it was right behind us,' I said. 'You do believe us, don't you?'

'Of course I believe you, Laura,' he said gravely.

'Then – what happened?' My voice faltered anxiously. 'Who knows!'

Again, the two drifting forms came to mind; the strange impression of strength they gave, of protection; two figures that could scarcely be seen.

'Are there ghosts in the mountains?' I asked.

Jean looked at me for a moment, very intently. '*Fantômes*?' he said, and then quietly, 'but of course. There is a legend, they tell in this region. They say that in the thirteenth century, the Cathars expelled one of their number; one of the "perfect" – the priests. He was accused of appalling crimes – stealing children among them. The Prince of Darkness had entered his soul, and he was executed. Before he died he vowed to return, and they say that, even now, long-dead Cathars guard the mountain passes, to keep young souls from harm.'

I shuddered, trying to close my mind against the image of Culfire, but I couldn't entirely banish it.

Milo had come in at the end of our conversation, but he had no time for talk of ghosts. His thoughts were all with Gwendal. He had just rung Mum to tell her we were coming home. Jean assured him that seats on a flight to Heathrow had already been booked.

'It will leave this evening,' Jean said, 'and Raoul will

take you. You have had enough driving, Milo. You must save your strength.'

For what, I wondered? Later his words would seem like a prophecy.

We had to leave soon after breakfast. As I stood by the door, gazing at the snowy peaks, I was already beginning to feel that I had not truly been here, that it was an imaginary interlude in my Christmas holidays, one that certainly wouldn't be believed by anyone I knew, except Mum, of course. Even Andy and Polly didn't know where I was, and they were probably having such a good time they wouldn't be interested.

We said goodbye to Jean and this time he and I kissed on both cheeks.

Raoul, already striding ahead, turned back to wave at Jean, and I said, 'You'll be all alone!'

'Yes, all alone again,' he said, as though it were inevitable. Perhaps, in spite of the hundreds of people he met in his pursuit of power he was really always alone, now more than ever. Gwendal had returned but chosen to leave.

'Milo!' he called after Dad. 'Send me word that he has come back!'

It sounded familiar and all at once I recognized the phrase. 'That's the last line of *The Little Prince*,' I said. 'The very last.'

Jean Tisseyre stared at me. 'Perhaps the last line has not yet been written.'

'Laura, we must go,' Dad shouted, and I had to run while Jean's expression printed itself in my mind forever.

Dad and I both fell asleep on the long drive to

Toulouse. Raoul had to wake us. His big smile had returned and he seemed glad to be sending us safely back home. I got two kisses from him and Milo was crushed in a bearhug.

'*Prenez-garde*! Take care!' Raoul kept repeating. He wouldn't leave us until we went through Passport Control.

Late that night we were standing outside our own front door, and the past three days seemed more than ever like a dream. Somehow I knew that Gwendal wasn't inside.

Mum had missed us. I'd never seen her quite so tearful. But after the big welcome home palaver, my parents disappeared into the living-room for Milo to give Mum a blow-by-blow account of our adventure. I could see they wanted privacy and I felt out of it, somehow, surplus to requirements, sort of thing. But I was too tired to be bothered by it, just then. Too worried about Gwendal.

On my way to bed I heard a strange cry coming from Andy's room, a cross between a squeak and a moan. I tore inside and saw Isidore lying on his back on the floor. The rats must have knocked him over. They were sitting by the open door of their cage, looking as if they wished they hadn't escaped. Isidore's squeak was growing louder.

I picked him up and set him on his feet. And then I saw the message. 'SHALL I COME BACK?'

'Gwendal!' I cried. I felt like saying, 'What a stupid question,' but the message I sent was more gentle. 'WE MISS YOU. YES, PLEASE COME BACK.'

7
The runaway returns

I ran downstairs with Isidore, and broke into my parents' intense discussion. They looked at me in consternation while I babbled on about Isidore and rats and messages.

'Start again, Laura!' Milo said.

So I left out the rats and just said, 'There's been a message from Gwendal.'

This worked much better. I told them I'd sent a message back. Milo took Isidore and began to press the keys.

'He hasn't replied yet,' I said.

'So we still don't know where he is,' Mum gave a big sigh.

I tried to keep my eyes open for a bit longer, but I was beginning to feel so sleepy I trundled off to bed and left them to it.

In the morning nothing had changed. Milo had slept with Isidore on the bedside table, but the robot-mobile had been silent all night, and his screen remained blank. Gwendal either wouldn't or couldn't send more information.

Mum paced the kitchen, irritably, putting sugar in the fridge and milk in the cupboard. Cross with herself for getting in a muddle, she said, 'He could have told us more. It's terrible not knowing.'

Milo tried to calm her down. 'He wouldn't upset us on purpose, Mary. He probably has a very good reason for remaining silent.'

It occurred to me that Isambard, not Gwendal, was at fault. I reminded Dad of the sinister image of water on the screen at Fort Saint-Luc. Perhaps Isambard had fallen in the lake at Château Mirande. The water could have damaged him.

'It's possible,' Milo declared. 'Good thinking, Lo!'

I was pleased to have contributed something at last, but my satisfaction didn't last long. When I thought of the water I began to see Gwendal on that precarious jetty, and then the other Gwendal, reaching for his spectacles and falling slowly.

'Suppose it isn't Gwendal at all,' I murmured. 'Suppose someone else has got hold of Isambard.'

Dad refused even to consider this, but I knew I'd sown a seed of doubt. I wished I hadn't.

That afternoon Polly came home with her best friend in tow. Jessica was to stay until school began again. Polly listened patiently to the descriptions of my exciting French holiday, but her eyes kept sliding over to Jessica, who wasn't the least bit interested. They spent the next two days closeted in one room or another, absorbed in their own games. It made me feel almost elderly.

Andy was a little more considerate. He arrived the day after Polly, looking more outdoors than ever. His face was sunburned and all his clothes smelled of pine. Even the whites of his eyes had acquired a tinge of Alpine blue.

I waited until after supper and then I followed him to his room and told him everything. I don't think I left out one little detail. He played with his rats while he listened, and although he whistled dutifully in all the right places, and arched his eyebrows and said 'Wow!' I felt he wasn't really with me. I began to think that because I wasn't telling it right, the story must seem untrue, or worse, that it was unexciting. Just before I reached the part where we'd seen the water appear on Isambard's screen, Andy suddenly remarked, 'Drift is almost as big as Snow, now!'

I nearly screamed 'You're too old to play with rats!' but I bit it back. I just gave a weary sigh and said, 'I'll tell you the rest some other time.' My three days and nights in France were slipping away from me, and I couldn't bear the loss. Even though my mind replayed every scene I could only make them real again if someone else could share it all with me. For three days I'd had Dad all to myself, but now he was out of reach. He shared his thoughts with Mum, not me.

There was someone who would have listened, but Isidore's screen remained blank, and every day Gwendal seemed more remote and less likely ever to come back. I couldn't stop imagining that the message had been a trick. Every day my suspicion strengthened. Gwendal was a prisoner somewhere, and couldn't escape.

I couldn't be bothered to get up early any more. Polly was usually the first one downstairs. She would give Lancelot his breakfast and then scrape the post from the front doormat. I was made aware of this when my parcel arrived. Polly opened my door and flung the package on to my pillow. I saw the French stamp and sat up, suddenly wide awake.

'What is it?' asked Polly.

'How should I know.' I tore off the paper.

Inside, there was a small leather-bound book. It was a French version of *The Little Prince*.

'*Le Petit Prince*,' I murmured, and held it up. 'Look, Polly!'

'Oh, a book,' she said. Jewels would have made a better impression, I suppose.

On the flyleaf he had written, 'To Laura, from your friend, Jean.' I fingered the soft green leather, wondering why he had sent it. And then I thought, Jean is the man in the story, the pilot stranded in the desert and waiting for word of the boy from a far planet. Perhaps I had reminded him of this when we said goodbye.

'How're you going to read it if it's in French?' asked Polly.

'I'll learn,' I said.

'Really?' She waltzed away, humming.

The night before the spring term began, I decided to make an effort with my school uniform. I washed and pressed and sewed. And then I had a go at Andy's. I can't think what came over me, but I could see that no one was going to do it if I didn't. Mum had been busy all week, and Dad was learning his lines for a new play.

I dragged the ironing board into my room and clamped my headphones over my ears. At least I could be enter-tained while I worked. At about four o'clock, my stomach began to groan for attention, so I went down to the kitchen.

And there he was.

I stood in the doorway, not quite believing what I saw. Gwendal, Polly and Jessica eating poached eggs while Dad poured cups of tea. As if nothing in the world had changed.

'Gwendal's back,' said Polly cheerfully.

'I can see that,' I muttered. 'Hullo, Gwendal!'

'Hi!' He looked up with a grin; a big, wide, healthy grin. He'd changed. I felt it at once. It wasn't just his long, wild hair or pink complexion. He was more robust and confident; older.

'I called you,' Milo said. 'Hungry?'

I nodded, frowning.

'We all called you,' Polly added, 'but we thought you were reading or finishing homework, or something.'

'I had my headphones on,' I said.

Gwendal's smile seemed fixed. He moved his chair so I could sit beside him.

'Where've you been?' I murmured. I couldn't think of anything else to say.

'All over,' he replied, rather jauntily.

'We've been asking,' said Polly, 'but he won't say, because he doesn't really know. He came on a plane to Heathrow, with a nice lady who had two children. He wasn't really with them, but everyone thought he was, so that was good, wasn't it? I wouldn't dare go on a plane by myself.'

'Nor me,' said Jessica, giving Gwendal an appraising glance. 'I wouldn't know how.'

'It's easy with a credit card,' said Gwendal coolly.

'I didn't know minors could have credit cards,' I muttered.

'My fa –' he looked at Milo, 'my guardian, I mean. He gave me one. He can do that sort of thing. He gave me loads of cash, too.'

Polly and Jessica had no difficulty accepting Gwendal's explanation. They wolfed down the remains of their tea and were off; back to Narnia or whatever world they had decided to live in that day.

'So aren't you going to tell us any more?' I asked, when the girls had gone.

Milo came and sat with us. 'All in good time,' he said.

'I want to know now,' I persisted. 'Because we've been everywhere, we've been in danger, and done the weirdest things and . . . and found out things, all because of you, Gwendal. And, by the way, what made you suddenly decide it was safe to live with us again?'

He was surprised by my outburst. 'You sent me a message,' he said.

'So, what took you so long?'

'I had to contact my . . . Jean,' he said. 'It took a long time because Isambard isn't working properly.'

'Ever heard of a phone box?' I sounded almost nasty. 'You could have phoned us, if you'd tried.'

'I don't like public telephones,' he said. 'You have to use money, and people watch you.'

It seemed ridiculous to me, that a boy who could book himself a plane ticket, couldn't use an ordinary phone box.

Milo gave me a reproving look and asked gently, 'What did Jean advise?'

'He told me there'd been an accident in the mountains,' said Gwendal, 'and that possibly Mr Culfire was gone for ever.'

'Possibly?' asked Milo.

'Probably,' said Gwendal. 'So I took a chance.'

'But what about Jean?' I asked.

Gwendal turned to me with a frown. 'I think he understood. He'll be busy, very busy soon. And he won't have time for me. Really, he wanted me to be here. But I'll be going to see him again at Easter, he says.'

'Can I come?' I found myself asking.

Gwendal looked surprised. 'That would be brilliant,' he said slowly. 'He likes you a lot.'

Milo suddenly leapt up, saying, 'Jean! I must tell him you're safe.'

'Let me speak first,' cried Gwendal.

They rushed out to the phone in the hall, and after a few brief, excited words, Gwendal gave the receiver to Dad.

He came back into the kitchen and sat beside me, and I began to feel guilty for giving him such a cool welcome. 'I'm glad you're back,' I said, 'really, really glad.'

Gwendal beamed at me. 'I am too.'

I told him about our visit to Château Mirande, and my meeting with Adèle, and how we knew that he had been there, in spite of everything Sophie said.

'I was,' he said. 'I climbed over a wall and walked through the wood and there it was – the lake and that long lawn up to the house. It looked empty but I didn't dare go any closer. I walked right round the lake and then ate my bread and cheese in a little hut in the wood. Later, when the light had gone, I went back to the lake for one last look.'

I asked him what his thoughts had been, as he stood by that dark water.

'I knew I'd come to the end of part of my life,' he said, 'the unhappy part. And I thought, now I can begin to be me. I looked into the water where that other boy had drowned and I felt . . .' he frowned with concentration, 'I can't explain how I felt. I let Isambard take a picture of the place, so that if I saw it again later, I might be able to understand. But I don't think I ever will. I just know that I feel better for it, not worse. I don't feel as if *I* had drowned there, you see, but that it was someone else. And I was sad for *him*, not me.'

'Weren't you scared? It must have been so dark.'

'There was moonlight, but when I stepped off the jetty, I dropped Isambard in the water. I couldn't find him for ages. He doesn't work too well, now. We never thought about making him waterproof.'

I thought of the small, drowned spectacles and shuddered.

Gwendal grinned. 'Really, I wasn't scared. I walked up to the house and slept in one of the stables. It was full of straw and very cosy. In the morning I ran back the way I'd come, through the woods, and when I climbed over the wall, a bus was arriving, on its way to Toulouse. I mean, how lucky can you get? It seemed like it was meant for me, that it was telling me I should go to the airport and come back to Milo, and all of you.'

'And you bought a plane ticket with a credit card?'

I must have sounded rather sceptical because he admitted that it hadn't really happened that way. He'd bought the ticket from a teenage backpacker. 'I paid him twice what it was worth,' Gwendal said proudly, 'so he was quite happy to make the deal.'

'Poor little rich boy,' I shook my head. 'You're loaded, aren't you?'

'Nope. It's nearly all gone. It was part of my Christmas present, but Jean said, "When it's gone, it's gone, so spend it wisely."'

'You did,' I said.

He gave me a thoughtful smile. 'It was a bit scary out there, sometimes, but it was such a good feeling, being ordinary, being in control. It won't ever change now, will it?'

Rashly, I promised that it wouldn't.

Milo was still on the phone when Mum arrived. She nearly collapsed when she saw Gwendal. Throwing down her briefcase (I'd never seen her do that before) she squeezed the poor boy half to death, chanting his name over and over.

He'd barely recovered when Andy came in. Andy's reaction was disappointing. 'Hi, Gwendal,' he said. 'So you're back. How's it been?'

'OK,' said Gwendal. And that was that.

Andy was becoming too cool by half.

At last Dad got off the phone. He had plenty to tell us. Sophie had left Château Mirande. She had indeed been guilty of passing on information. Culfire's search for Gwendal had led, inevitably, to the château. He had met Sophie and offered her a small fortune to let him know if ever she saw Gwendal. And when she had seen him, greed and fear drove her to call Nathan Culfire. But Gwendal was on a bus to Toulouse by the time he arrived. So he waited, and followed us instead, believing we would lead him to his angel.

'And the grey car?' I asked. 'What really happened?'

'There *was* an accident,' Milo said. 'Gérard swore that he and his friends had nothing to do with it. It occurred on that treacherous bend, just before we met them. The car was coming too fast on the frozen snow. It went into a skid, crashed through the wall on the verge and plunged a hundred feet.'

'And the driver?' Mum asked.

Milo glanced at Gwendal. 'Didn't stand a chance.' he said. 'The engine exploded.'

'Was it Culfire?' For Gwendal's sake I had to know.

'Probably. But after a fire it's hard to tell.'

So that was that. End of chapter. None of us wanted to talk about it any more. We could put it behind us. Dad got out a bottle of wine and Andy was sent to buy vast quantities of kebabs at the Greek takeaway. The McCools toasted their New Year, and their new lives.

I was still licking my fingers when Gwendal made his announcement. He wanted to go to school. He'd enjoyed being free so much, he wanted to stay 'out' as he put it.

'I'll be safer in school,' he pointed out. 'And it's time I socialized properly.'

So it was agreed. Next morning Milo phoned Polly's headteacher and then Jean. It was surprising how easy it was. Gwendal had a place in school, and documents would be compiled and forwarded. He would be given a number – an existence. He would truly belong to our family.

The following day, we set off together. All four of us, plus Milo. A real family at last. We parted at the crossroads, Andy and I walking on to the comprehensive, Milo taking Polly and Gwendal round to the primary.

On his very first day at school, Gwendal made a friend. His name was Joe Romayne and, according to Polly, he was big for his age but all right. He wasn't too rough and he wasn't a bully. His nickname was Jimbo.

Before the end of the week, Jimbo and Gwendal were visiting each other. We met Mrs Romayne, who seemed perfectly normal (a bit talkative for my liking, but you can't have everything) and Jimbo was going to sleep over at the weekend.

I should have been happy for Gwendal. Everyone else was. But something was weighing me down, a sort of heaviness in my head which dragged on the muscles that helped me to smile.

Dad must have noticed my lack of smiles because one evening he remarked, 'You're very solemn these days, Lo!'

'Am I?'

'What is it? An overload of homework?'

I had to face it, but it hurt to bring the problem into the open, even though it was just for Milo.

'I haven't got any friends,' I said. 'It didn't seem to matter when Gwendal was . . . like he used to be, but now I feel the odd one out.'

'Oh, Lo!' Dad came and gave me a hug. 'It won't last. You're too good for them all, that's your problem.'

'Problem, yes!' I said.

I didn't know that Marie-Claire was just around the corner. I found her in the school library, or rather she found me. Her name was Marie-Claire Perrin, her mother was from Zaire, her father was French. She was just about the most perfect being I'd ever seen and why she chose me was a mystery. (She told me later that it was because I looked hostile yet interesting? Me?)

One minute I had my head in a book, the next I was watching this amazing person walk towards me, smiling. She was tall and dark with loads of glistening black hair and the sort of features you see on African carvings. She sat down opposite me and said 'How're you doin'?' as if she'd known me all her life.

My mouth swung open. 'I . . . I'm OK,' I said. 'Who are you?'

'Marie-Claire.'

'I'm Laura.'

'I just got here,' she said. 'Bit late, huh? Can you tell me a few things?'

'I'll try,' I said, already enchanted by her accent.

We discovered we were in the same year but different classes, and the few things she wanted to know were put on hold while she gave me a brief synopsis of her life. When I began to talk about my family I found myself telling the funniest bits, especially about Milo. Marie-Claire had a laugh with musical notes in it. It lifted my own, much neglected, laugh right out of me and up to the ceiling. People kept looking at us and saying 'Sssh!'

By the end of our lunch break it seemed as though we'd always been friends. And at last I found I could talk about my time in France.

Marie-Claire's dark eyes grew very wide, and she listened, really listened. I couldn't tell her the whole truth, of course. Even she might have found that hard to take. It was enough just to be able to describe our extraordinary journey, and the fort that belonged to our good friend. To Marie-Claire Gwendal was my brother, and she didn't even remark on the lack of resemblance when she met him.

Life was set fair to be wonderful. Better than any of us could have hoped. I should have known it couldn't last. You see we'd reckoned without the last wolf.

8

The final bite

At the beginning of February, an arctic winter descended on us. Huge, feathery snowflakes settled on our shoulders as we came home from school. Mountain snow, I called it, and Marie-Claire laughed. 'You've got mountains on the brain,' she said.

By the time I got home there was an inch of snow lying in the garden. At tea-time we left the curtains open so that we could watch the snowflakes whirling past the window. It made me think of our ghostly mountain guardians. Perhaps, if they'd been outside, hidden in our English snow, events wouldn't have turned out the way they did.

I stayed up later than usual. I had a pile of homework to finish, but the weather was a terrible distraction. Andy and Gwendal began to build a snowman in the back garden, and I kept stopping to watch them.

At about nine o'clock I went to make myself a mug of cocoa. I was just passing through the hall when the doorbell rang. So I opened the door.

He wasn't on rollerblades, or wearing a black balaclava, but I knew our visitor. Even though he wasn't the one with cold, unforgettable eyes, fear ran through my veins like oil, and my fingers kept slipping away from the door handle.

'I want to speak to Mr McCool,' he said.

I tried to say, 'You must be joking,' but my lips were numb.

'Please,' he said. 'It's really urgent.'

'Dad!' I croaked. 'There's someone here.'

Milo came out of the living-room. He didn't recognize the man immediately. 'Yes?' he said.

'I have to talk to you.' He had rather a thin voice and he wasn't so big without his blades. He had a very unhealthy complexion.

Dad came up behind me. 'What's it about?' he asked.

'Culfire!' It sounded like a password.

'You'd better come in,' Milo said.

He took the young man into the kitchen and I followed, naturally. Mum came in and stood by the sink, propping herself against the draining-board.

He told us his name was Adam Hawkins and he was sorry for all the trouble he'd caused, but his mate, Paul, had led him into it. They'd done it for cash, initially, but Paul was a bit of a sadist. He'd begun to enjoy tormenting people, especially little kids. Adam hadn't liked that. 'It was a coward's game, and I didn't want no part of it,' he said.

When Culfire and Paul went to France, Adam stayed behind. 'An' I'm bloody glad I did. 'Cos Paul got it, didn't he?' He pulled out a chair and sat down, elbows on the table.

'Got it?' Mum enquired.

' 'Ad an accident – car crash!' Adam replied. 'Could I have a glass of water?'

Milo whipped round but Mum beat him to it. She put the glass on the table. Milo sat next to Adam. 'Where?' he asked. 'Where was this accident?'

'In the mountains. It was 'orrible. The car exploded.'

'How d'you know all this?' Mum sat down, too.

I stayed by the door, quiet as a mouse, so no one would notice and tell me I should be in bed.

'I know, 'cos Culfire told me.' Adam rubbed his spotty cheek. 'He was with him, you see, with Paul when the car went over. But Culfire got out. Don't ask me how.'

'Luck of the devil,' Dad murmured.

Adam looked at Milo. 'Funny you should say that,' he said. 'Culfire isn't his real name, you know. It's a . . . an anagram.'

Mum and Dad must have worked it out at exactly the same time. They stared at each other, Mum frowning, Dad's eyes growing round.

'Lucifer,' Dad murmured.

'Yeah!' Adam looked impressed. 'That angel that got sent to 'ell.'

'The bearer of light,' Dad said. 'He thought himself equal to God.'

'Daft, isn't it?' mumbled Adam.

'No, I don't think it's daft,' Mum said. 'It's horrible.'

'And why have you come to tell us all this?' Milo asked. 'Have you had a sudden change of heart, or what?'

' 'E threatened me. I didn't want no more of it, but 'e said if I didn't do what he asked, 'ed let me 'ave it, said I'd better watch out when I crossed the road, or stood too near a railway line.' Adam gulped down his water and slammed the glass on the table. 'I thought I'd tell you all this,' he went on, 'so you could go to the police. They'd believe you.'

Milo ran his hands through his hair. 'What exactly did Culfire want you to do?' he asked.

'Get the kid and take him to the Society. It's an old 'ouse in North London. You go up a load of steps and there's this 'orrible grey place. It looks empty – all boarded up where the ivy 'asn't covered it. But 'e's in there. And I don't know what else.'

I shuddered and Dad looked up, suddenly realizing I was there. But it was too late for him to send me away. I wish Adam had stopped talking then, but now he'd started he couldn't stop.

' 'E's got a thing about your kid,' he said grimly. ' 'E says 'e's an angel. Don't ask me why. 'E's crazy, you know. Bonkers.'

'And the Society?' asked Milo. 'How many of them are there?'

'Culfire *is* the Society. It folded, 'e said. 'E's the only one left. No one else. Just 'im. It kind of made 'im worse I reckon. 'E wants to keep the kid isolated. Wants to see how long 'e'll last in the dark . . .'

'All right,' Dad said. 'We get the picture.'

It was too late. I heard the breathless little gasp even before Milo scraped back his chair, saying, 'That's enough, Adam!'

I glanced through the half-open door, just in time to see Gwendal creeping upstairs.

Adam looked confused. He obviously wanted to tell us more, but Mum and Dad wouldn't let him.

'We appreciate you coming here,' said Milo, 'and I'm

going to do my best to see that you're safe. But I think you ought to go now.'

'Are you going to the police?' Adam pleaded in a whiney voice.

Dad glanced at Mum. 'We'll see.'

' 'E'll get someone else to do it,' Adam warned. Dad followed him as he slouched to the front door. 'There's some that'll do anything for cash.'

'I'm sure,' said Milo. 'Just give me the address, please.'

'The Society? It's number thirteen, Woodville Avenue, Northwick.'

'Thank you.' Milo opened the door. 'Try not to worry, Adam. And please don't tell anyone else about all this.'

'As if I would.' He stepped out and Dad closed the door.

Mum came and took both my hands. 'I wish you hadn't heard all that, Laura. You're not to worry. You must go to bed and forget it.'

'How can I?' I said, and lowering my voice I added, 'Gwendal heard, too.'

'What?' Mum looked appalled.

'Gwendal?' Dad said.

I told them about the tiny gasp that gave him away, and how I'd seen him creeping up the stairs, after the very worst of Adam's news.

'Listen, Lo,' Dad said solemnly. 'You mustn't think about this any more. We'll sort it out tomorrow. Try and get some sleep, OK?'

I nodded. What else could I do? I was so exhausted I even forgot my cocoa. I wandered off to bed and lay there, listening to my parents murmuring through the night. I could guess what they were saying. Mum would be all for telling the police, 'outing' Gwendal at last and facing the consequences. And perhaps she was right. Would it really make so much difference to Gwendal? Dad wouldn't take the chance. He would choose the dangerous route. Somehow, I would have to help him, but I fell asleep before I could make any plans.

The change in Gwendal was dramatic. He sat at the breakfast table with a white face, unable to eat. Dad took Andy aside and told him what had happened. But we left Polly out of it. We didn't want to ruin everybody's day.

The snow on the lawn had frozen to a thick crust, and it was icy cold. We began to pile on our scarves and coats and gloves, but Gwendal didn't move.

'Come on, Gwendal,' Milo said.

'I'm not going to school,' he muttered. 'I'm ill.'

'No. You're not. You're fine,' Dad told him.

Mum still hovered in the hall. She should have left for work at least half an hour ago. But she was obviously afraid to leave Dad in charge.

'It's all right, Mary,' he said brusquely. 'Go to work. Now. It's just a normal day. We're not going to let this thing get to us.'

'What thing?' asked Polly.

'Tell you later,' I said quietly.

Gwendal looked at me and I couldn't bear the misery in his wide blue eyes. He was right back where he started. A frightened and bewildered boy who didn't know who he was. But now it was worse because for a while he'd known what it was like to be ordinary. He knew what he could lose.

Polly came to the rescue. 'Jimbo will want to know

what's happened to you. You're his best friend.'

Gwendal showed a spark of interest, and Andy took advantage of this. 'I'll come all the way into school with you, if you like,' he said. 'And I'll come right in to fetch you. You'll be much safer there, than in here.'

'Much,' agreed Polly, without knowing the full story.

Gwendal grabbed a slice of toast and stood up.

'Mary, it'll be all right,' Dad said carefully. 'Go on!'

Mum gave us all a kiss and then she was gone. We shoved Gwendal into his coat, wound a scarf round his neck, and set off. An ordinary family, on an ordinary day. The worst day of my life.

I met Marie-Claire in the lunch break. I'd had a pre-moni-tion. 'I'm going home,' I told her. 'Will you let them know? I've got History next lesson. Tell Miss Leith I'm ill.'

'Are you?' She immediately looked concerned.

'Not really,' I confessed. 'It's something I've got to do at home. Family problems. Tell you later.'

'OK,' she said. 'You take care, now.'

I promised her I would, then I ran all the way home. I was just in time. Milo had dragged his motorbike out of the garage. The old Norton stood on the icy path, every inch of chrome and metal shining.

'Where are you going?' I asked, knowing full well. 'Why don't you use the train, or a bus?'

'And why are you here?' he sighed.

I told him I'd guessed what he was going to do. 'Please don't go up there, Dad,' I begged. 'I've got this really, really bad feeling about it. The police can sort Culfire out.'

'I'm just going to warn him,' he said. 'Threaten him if you like. If it doesn't work then, yes, I suppose we'll have to tell the police. But they may not believe us, and then where will we be?'

In my quietest voice, I said, 'Perhaps he really is Lucifer.'

'Don't be silly, Lo!'

I followed him into the house and crept upstairs in his shadow. I stood by the door of his room and watched him put on his leather jacket, buckling the straps and fastening the studs. I felt like a squire attending his knight before battle. I should carry the armour, I thought, the breastplate or the lance. But he only gave me a gauntlet to hold. He pulled on his long leather boots and then a black helmet, over his wild silver hair. I trailed him into the garden again, neither of us speaking. He wheeled the Norton onto the road and swung himself into the saddle. When I passed him the gauntlet he gave me a big smile, then pushed down his visor. I couldn't say a word. Our Dark Knight kicked his charger, and with a bellow, she carried him away.

I dashed back to lock the door, then ran all the way to the station. A train had just pulled in and I jumped on seconds before the doors closed. I had two changes to make before I got to Northwick.

The journey seemed endless. I kept closing my eyes and counting the minutes. It was impossible to guess how long it would take a motorbike to cover the same distance. I had to wait for ages at the second station and when the train finally came in, it was stationary for at least five minutes.

When I got out at Northwick it was almost four o'clock. The clouds were thick and dark and the temperature had dropped to zero. The melted snow had turned to treacherous ice again.

'Woodville Avenue?' The paper-seller outside the station scratched his woollen hat. 'That's miles, darlin'. A good half-hour's walk.'

My heart sank but he gave me very precise directions, grunting into the wind while I swung from foot to foot on the frosty pavement.

I set off. A hundred yards up the High Street. Turn left. A long walk now, through the town. I didn't realize how hilly it was in north London. We live south of the river. It's warmer there, I'm sure. Or is it just that houses look colder at a higher altitude? The frost hadn't budged all day. Trees, hedges, walls were all a dull, mean white.

In Woodville Avenue, people hurried past me all in one direction, or so it seemed. As if they were hastening from the scene of a crime. Their faces were tucked into collars, or swathed in scarves.

The Norton was parked outside number thirteen. Like a landmark. The house was just as Adam had described it: grey, gloomy, the sort of house with high ceilings and echoing corridors. The name on the gate looked as if it had been burnt into the wood with a hot poker. 'The Society for Angels'. I walked through the gate and faced the mountain of glassy steps.

Above the peeling front door there was a window with a balcony. The window was boarded with thin planks of wood, and the balcony had lost most of the columns that supported its low wall.

I was halfway up the steps when I heard the scream: a chilling, inhuman sound, not Milo's, it rose to a terrifying wail, and then came the crash and the tearing, splintering sound of bodies exploding through wood. As I looked up they tumbled over the balcony and a black cloud of limbs fell to earth. There was a sickening thud as gravity hugged them. An impact that you know must have death in it. And then nothing.

As I moved my scream ripped through the silence. 'Dad! Dad! Dad!'

The street stopped rushing past. I could feel them scrambling up the steps and clustering behind me, caught by my scream.

I reached the black bundle and fell beside it. They lay side by side. Milo's arm was still held in the wolf's claw. A dark pool was already forming round the two heads. Culfire had fallen face down, Milo was on his side. He had always known how to fall, had my dad. I flung my arm round him and lay as close as I could.

Someone with a mobile began to call an ambulance. Kind hands touched my hair, patted my shoulder, tried to prise me away from my father, but I clung on fiercely. I wouldn't let him leave me.

When the ambulance arrived I allowed them to take care of him. The bodies were lifted on to stretchers and carried down the perilous steps. It was awkward and dangerous. I scrambled after them, keeping Milo's face in my sight. The other face was covered. They let me travel with Dad; already he was being fixed to a drip. Everyone looked so grave, so anxious to do the right thing.

In spite of the shock, I was ready when the police began gently to question me. For Milo's sake I had to get it right, otherwise his battle would have been for nothing.

And who would believe a story about stolen angels.

'It was drugs,' I told them. 'Mr Culfire was pushing drugs. We couldn't prove it so my father decided to – investigate. (As a matter of fact drugs were exactly what they found when they went into the house. No one ever discovered who Culfire really was.)

By some miracle, Mum had come up with the same story. She arrived at the hospital crumpled and pale. I'd never seen her look so helpless. We sat side by side, my fingers squeezed tight in hers, and waited. And waited and waited.

At some time during that long watch, I found myself asking, 'Why did he do it, Mum? When he knew he might end up giving his life away?'

She gave me a grim little smile. 'He couldn't help himself. Some people are like that.'

'Are they? I can't think of any others. Can you?'

'No.' She began to murmur, very softly, and I thought she was talking to herself and then I realized it was something she wanted me to know. She was telling me about a certain day, thirteen years ago. She'd been walking home from a late-night party. Dawn was breaking and she decided to stroll beside the river. When she was approaching Chelsea Bridge, she noticed a film crew on the bank. The director was shouting across the water and as she watched a man leapt off the bridge. She had known immediately, that it was one of the Dark Knights.

Mum turned to me, and I saw that her eyes were shining with tears. 'As he leapt, sunlight spilled over the water, and I found I couldn't get my breath,' she gave a funny little laugh. 'I felt as though he'd leapt into my heart. Does that sound silly, Lo?'

'Oh, no,' I breathed. 'It sounds perfect.' And I knew she'd never told a soul about that moment, not even Milo. I knew I'd found the real Mary. Everything she'd ever done had been for him.

There was nothing we could do at the hospital. They told us to go home. Milo was in safe hands, stable but not out of danger. Tomorrow, there'd be better news. Perhaps.

Andy had cooked supper and taken care of things at home, but he was relieved to see us. Mum was impressed and grateful. They clustered round her, Polly, Gwendal and Andy, begging for news. She told them what she knew, and then they turned to me.

When Gwendal heard that Culfire was dead, he gave such a joyful smile I wanted to shake him. What about Milo, I wanted to cry? But, really I was glad that he was safe. He had always known that Milo would save him.

Mum rang the hospital early next morning. There was no change, they said. Milo was in a coma. We had to go to school and pretend that life was normal. Mum went to the hospital. She told us Dad looked peaceful, but was still asleep. On her pale skin, the worry lines had sunk so deep I couldn't imagine how they would ever be erased.

I asked if I could see Dad and Mum agreed to take me. But the others wouldn't go. I was shocked and angry. Were they scared, I asked? Andy mumbled that it wouldn't help and Mum told me not to push it. It wasn't necessary.

So it was just Mum and me. Milo looked like a ghost.

His arm was in plaster and there were tubes going into his nose and everywhere. He had a bandage on his head and his closed lids were like bruises. Mum talked to him and held his hand, but I just stood beside her, watching. I couldn't touch him.

There was no change in the night. Without Marie-Claire I don't know how I would have coped. I told her everything, almost everything. And she sat with me in every break and listened. I'd taken a book to school with me and I asked her, 'D'you think if I read to my dad, it would help?'

'Yeah! It's what they do, isn't it?' she said. 'They read stories to people in comas.'

'I'll go straight after school, then, by myself. Then he'll have an hour with me, and an hour with Mum.'

'It's a great idea,' Marie-Claire approved. 'Who knows, maybe he'll hear you, and wake up.'

I told Andy my plan and ran to the bus stop as soon as the school bell went.

The nurses were very kind. They gave me a chair and I sat close to Dad and, for the first time, I held his hand. It was cool and heavy and it frightened me. I began to read the book I'd brought with me, The Little Prince.

He gave no sign that he could hear me. Behind his blue eyelids there wasn't a flicker, and the only sound he made was a distant, hollow, breathing. When I left I felt helpless and tearful.

The following afternoon Milo had another visitor. Jean Tisseyre had flown over from France, incognito, of course. Mum found him at the hospital but I didn't see him. He didn't want to arouse curiosity by coming to the house. I knew he would do all he could to help us. He certainly managed to raise Mum's spirits.

I went to the hospital again, next day, and read another few chapters. There were twenty-seven of them. Gradually I lost my fear of the lifeless hand, but the vacant face and motionless body filled me with despair.

Milo used to say, 'Knock! Knock! Is anyone there?' when he caught me day-dreaming.

Was he day-dreaming? 'Knock! Knock! Dad! Are you there? Knock! Knock! Tell me the last wolf didn't get you, Milo!'

Mum finally persuaded the others to go with her, while I went round to Marie-Claire's house. When I got back I found the whole family looking scared and depressed. Mum said, 'I don't think we'll try that again.'

On my third visit to the hospital I read to the middle of chapter twenty-six. But I couldn't go on. I didn't dare. I'd begun to think The Little Prince was a kind of spell, and if I reached the end and Dad still hadn't woken up, then he never would.

One of the nurses came and put an arm round me. 'You know he's in very good shape,' she said. 'Apart from his arm, nothing is broken. If he wakes up he'll be as good as new. It's a miracle, really.'

I wished she hadn't said if. 'It's not quite a miracle,' I murmured.

She smiled ruefully and walked away. A rippling grey mist took her place. Creatures with pointed ears and feathery tails. I felt their coarse coats brush against me, and heard the gentle clatter of their claws. They gathered round my father's bed and pressed their snouts against the covers, gazing at him. But their yellow eyes held no malice, rather they seemed to regret what had befallen Milo.

'Laura, wake up!' The nurse was back again. 'You're falling asleep, love. You ought to go home.'

That evening I found myself screaming. I was babbling about wolves and angels, about knights on black horses and little princes. I couldn't stop. At the back of my mind, I could see them pulling out the tubes that held my father to earth, and letting him float away.

Mum had to shout to get through to me. 'Stop it, Laura! Stop it! You must climb out of those stories. We need you here!' She hugged me very tight, and although I knew the hug was meant for Milo, it was comforting to be included in it.

Later, when I was reading in bed, there was a knock on my door and Gwendal looked in.

'What is it?' I asked, rather coldly.

He came and sat on the end of my bed. 'D'you want me to come with you tomorrow?' he asked. 'When you go and see Dad?'

'Would you?' I said. 'Would you really come, Gwendal?'

'Of course. I've been wanting to. But I'm a coward.'

'No, you're not,' I said. 'I'll fetch you from school. OK?'

'OK. Night then.' He tiptoed back to bed.

I thought about Gwendal's cold, clinical beginning. He wasn't Jean's beloved drowned boy, after all. He never could be. He was my father's son. Did he realize, at last, how much he was loved?

I was so relieved that I wouldn't be alone when I read that last chapter, for the first time in ages I slept the whole night through.

The nurses were pleased to see two of us. They gave us a chair each and we sat on either side of the bed. Gwendal looked across at me and whispered, 'I've brought another book, for when we finish yours.'

'You don't have to whisper,' I said. 'He likes to hear voices.'

Gwendal stared doubtfully at Milo's unconscious face.

'That's what they say.' As I opened the book, I silently asked Antoine de Saint-Exupéry to help me. I read very slowly, from the place where the little prince decides to let the snake bite him, so that his body will be light enough to travel back to his own planet. Gwendal listened intently. When I came to the end of the chapter, he said, 'Go on!'

I couldn't get past the first sentence of chapter twenty-seven. It was such a short chapter, and the end of the book so near. My voice was thick and the words kept slipping away from me.

'Shall I read it?' Gwendal asked.

I passed the book over Milo's unmoving arms.

The words sounded strange in Gwendal's thin little voice, but he was a competent reader and after a while the story seemed to belong to him. Then he turned the last page and panic set in. I couldn't breathe. I couldn't hear the words. I tried to stop him, to explain that if he came to the end of the book, the world might end, too. But I couldn't speak. And Gwendal's voice flowed on.

So I took the lifeless hand in mine and clung to it. And

the hand seemed to know that I was there. I hardly dared to glance at his face, but when I did, I found that Milo's eyes were open, and he was smiling.

EGMONT PRESS: ETHICAL PUBLISHING

Egmont Press is about turning writers into successful authors and children into passionate readers – producing books that enrich and entertain. As a responsible children's publisher, we go even further, considering the world in which our consumers are growing up.

Safety First
Naturally, all of our books meet legal safety requirements. But we go further than this; every book with play value is tested to the highest standards – if it fails, it's back to the drawing-board.

Made Fairly
We are working to ensure that the workers involved in our supply chain – the people that make our books – are treated with fairness and respect.

Responsible Forestry
We are committed to ensuring all our papers come from environmentally and socially responsible forest sources.

For more information, please visit our website at
www.egmont.co.uk/ethicalpublishing